Wannabe

Wannabe

SHELLEY STOEHR

Delacorte Press

Published by
Delacorte Press
Bantam Doubleday Dell Publishing Group, Inc.
1540 Broadway
New York, New York 10036

Library of Congress Cataloging-in-Publication Data

Stoehr, Shelley.
    Wannabe / Shelley Stoehr.
        p.   cm.
    Summary: Catherine's dream of someday moving beyond her life in Little Italy is jeopardized by her older brother's ambition to join the local mobsters and her own involvement with some unsavory characters, leading them both into using cocaine.
    ISBN 0-385-32223-2 (alk. paper)
    [1. Brothers and sisters—Fiction. 2. Italian Americans—Fiction. 3. Cocaine habit—Fiction. 4. Drug abuse—Fiction.
5. Little Italy (New York, N.Y.)—Fiction.]   I. Title.
PZ7.S8695Wan   1997
[Fic]—dc20   96-21699
                                                   CIP
                                                   AC

The text of this book is set in 13.5-point Adobe Garamond.
Book design by Julie E. Baker

Manufactured in the United States of America
March 1997
10 9 8 7 6 5 4 3 2 1
BVG

To Bone

Wannabe

Chapter One

"Hooker boots!" Mickey called them, before I slammed my bedroom door in his face.

I couldn't tell if he was seriously angry, or just kidding with me. I didn't have time to deal with him either way, if I was still going to get to work on time. Mickey wouldn't understand about that.

Sliding the red leather up and over my knees, I wanted to scream from the power trip. The soft, new-smelling leather reached almost to my crotch, and the spiked heels felt like weapons. I hated to take them off, but I couldn't leave home looking so good.

New boots and minidress tucked into my backpack, I sneaked toward the front door. Ma was still at her job, and Pop was sleeping, again. But Mickey had come home early—usually he didn't show until Ma had dinner on the table. I didn't want to explain about my job to him, yet.

"Yo, Sis!" he yelled from the kitchen as I passed.

Swallowing hard, I peeked in. There was a bottle of Southern Comfort on the table, which

1

Mickey insisted on drinking, even though I told him it was a girl's drink. Mickey sat at the head of the table, dealing cards. Three of his dumber buddies were scattered around, leaning back on two legs of their chairs, accidents waiting to happen.

Mickey smiled. "Joe wants to see those new boots you got."

The Three Stooges laughed, until Mickey smacked the one nearest to him across the nose.

"It wasn't *that* funny," Mickey said. "That's my sister, you know."

While he was glaring at his friend, I hurried to the door. As I shut it behind me, I heard him say in his exaggerated tough-guy voice, "Hey, Catherine, what'd you get them boots for any-way?"

"To kick you with!" I yelled back, and heard him laugh.

I got in a cab quickly and asked the driver to take me to Mulberry and Prince. He looked at me funny because it was only three blocks away. I glared at him until he shrugged and drove.

Chapter Two

People think New York is such a big city. But between the old men in their beach chairs on the sidewalk, the old women leaning out their windows, and the young wannabe mobsters in the doorways, my neighborhood might as well have been Bumfuck, Iowa, for all the privacy I had. Maybe there really is a God, because somehow, Ma, Pop and Mickey still didn't know where I worked. Course, if there was a God, I wouldn't be spending Friday and Saturday nights as a cocktail waitress in Little Italy.

Since I couldn't completely trust God's discretion, I used my own evasive tactics to confuse anyone who might be watching me. When I got out of the cab, I walked over one block to Lafayette Street, then up to Bleecker, which was out of my neighborhood altogether, then across two blocks to Elizabeth, then back down to Prince, and finally onto Mott. I ducked quickly into Gatto's.

That wasn't really the name of the social club where I worked—it didn't have a name. But I called it Gatto's to myself, because *gatto* means cat in Italian. Mario, the owner, looked like one.

He was sitting at the bar as I came in. Squinting against the sudden rush of sunlight coming through the open door, he hissed at me. I pulled the door shut behind me quickly. As I hurried past, he grabbed my arm. I wanted to tell him he needed to be declawed.

"How's your brother?" he purred, relaxing his grip.

I felt a cool breeze inside my chest, because he mentioned Mickey, and also because in the month since I'd started at Gatto's, this was the first time Mario had even spoken to me.

He laughed coarsely. Clawing my backside in a shriveled attempt at a pat on the rear, he gestured with his head toward the kitchen.

"Go get pretty," said Paulie from behind the bar.

I relaxed a little. It was normal for Paulie to do Mario's talking. The encounter with Mario had been like a little dance in the Twilight Zone, but I was back in my own dimension now.

Actually, when I really thought about it, working at Gatto's was always a little Twilight Zone–ish, just because I worked there *at all*. It wasn't the typical job for a nice girl like me. I was supposed to work at McDonald's or Grand Union, or something. Only that would be *so uncool.* Gatto's was dangerous and wild. Actually, more action probably went down at a McDonald's in New York City, but an Italian social club made the *news.* I was a part of *history!*

I fixed my makeup quickly in the kitchen. If I didn't get the false eyelashes on before the sun set, it would be too dark to get them on straight. Joe, the cook, was almost blind, so the only light in the kitchen came from a greasy, tobacco-colored lightbulb hanging above the cutting board.

Although I probably could have changed clothes openly in the kitchen without Joe noticing or caring—he never even acknowledged that I existed—I went into the big pantry and pulled the curtain-door closed. Joe was humming "Nobody Knows the Trouble I Seen," which might be his true story. It would explain why his eyelids were puckered with pink-white scar tissue, with just a little filmy crack open at the bottom to see through, if he could see at all. Most of his face, and part of his scalp, looked like that too.

Paulie told me Joe was burned working the french-fryer at McDonald's when he was about my age. Yeah, whatever.

After I finished dressing, I got out my wig, which I kept twisted like a snake in a small bag. The twisting helped it keep its curl. Since it wasn't a full wig but blended with my own hair to make it look longer, I had to put rubber bands in the front and back of my own hair, so that the combs that held the wig on would have something to grab. It hurt like hell to make it tight enough that it couldn't possibly come loose, but I felt more comfortable wearing it. Especially since longer hair meant better tips.

Satisfied with my new look, I went back out into the club. It wasn't busy yet, but Mario was stationed at his usual back table, surrounded by eight admirers. Paulie stopped on his way over to bring them drinks and passed the tray to me.

"Tell Joe, extra garlic, and better use the linguini noodles tonight," Paulie said as he shuffled back to the bar.

Two young greaseballs were yammering to Mario as I set down the drinks. One was Mario's nephew, Frankie. He looked like a cat, too, but slicker and fatter than Mario. He looked like my grandmother's old tabby, who used to spend the morning prowling through garbage in the alley and then come inside licking his chops and proud, like he'd slain some rats, when in fact all he'd conquered was an open can of tuna. Then he'd spend the rest of the day lounging on top of the radiator, swishing his fat tail at you and hissing if you got too close.

Mario looked bored, but he didn't tell the twerp to get lost. I couldn't either, no matter how much Frank swished his tail at me. He wiggled his fat ass a little for my benefit when I got close, but didn't move aside, so I had to squeeze between him and the wall to get Mario's old-fashioned to him. As I leaned over, Frankie's entourage whistled. Mario looked at them like he was going to spit blood through his eyes, and they shut up real fast.

"Yo, Mario," Frankie said, "don't bust on dem. We did a hard bit of work today . . ."

This time, Mario did spit. Saliva dripped off Frank's forehead, but even a punk like him knew better than to wipe it off before Mario was through with him.

"Am I your mother's brother?" Mario said.

Frankie nodded. I squeezed out of the tight spot between Frankie and the wall. Being so close to Mario when he was talking gave me goose bumps. As I unloaded the rest of the drinks from my tray, I was careful not to look up.

Mario continued, "Then you call me *Uncle* Mario, and then you shut the fuck up. And quit talking like a goddamn street punk. I *know* they teach you proper English in school, and I also know you don't talk like that at home."

I knew Frankie must be sweating, and it made me feel good. Maybe he'd stop strutting around the neighborhood like he was the fucking Godfather, when everyone knew Mario and his boys wouldn't trust Frankie to tie their shoelaces for them, much less do any real work.

Someone pinched my behind as I moved away from the table. Trying not to glare, in case it was someone important, or someone with money, I looked up. Fuckin' A, it was just one of Frankie's "bodyguards." He had no neck, and no brain, and he was in my sex education class in school. He blew spitballs from the back of the room, and the girls in the front row always giggled nasally through their fake noses. They believed him when he said he was in the Mafia and was gonna get made when he graduated.

Oh, please. His mother wasn't even Italian.

Grinning at Tony like I was just another one of the bimbettes from the front row of sex class, I tried to move away. He grabbed my shoulder and leaned forward to whisper in my ear. He didn't even smell like garlic, he smelled like a hamburger.

"Maybe we'll get together later," he said.

Yeah, right, I thought. I realized he didn't recognize me from school. I was glad for my wig and slutty outfit. I grinned again and walked quickly back to the bar. Suddenly I knew I was bigger than all of them put together. They were lame high-school wannabes, and I was the only woman allowed in Mario's club. A short skirt is a wonderful thing.

After wiping the tray clean, I headed to the kitchen to tell Joe about linguini and extra garlic. Suddenly I heard a loud hiss, then a bang. I froze, then slowly turned.

The hiss was Mario. The bang was a beer bottle being slammed onto the table. Froth spilled over the bottle's lip like a volcano. Frankie's olive complexion had turned to gray.

"Paulie!" Mario said. "Are you feeding my nephew beer?"

Paulie knew better than to answer that Frankie always drank when he was here—usually Mario ordered beers all around for Frankie and his friends and bodyguards.

"This is my sister's son!" Mario said. "You know he's barely eighteen? If you know that, why are you serving him booze? You want me to get closed down? You want my sister to call me up three in the morning, when her son comes home piss-ass drunk?"

All the other boys had put their beers down, and when Paulie nodded at me, I went over and started clearing. Paulie followed me with a rag. As he wiped the table, he whispered something in Mario's ear that seemed to calm him down.

While I waited for Paulie to fill eight soda glasses for Frankie and his entourage, I took deep breaths, like they taught in that yoga class I took at the YMCA. Working Gatto's Friday nights was a lesson in self-control. And it was still early. I wished Mario would go to an old-age home already. Or at least get out his folding beach chair and relax on the sidewalk with everyone else his age. He was getting kookier every week.

Some men sitting at the bar were elbowing each other and laughing.

"Stupid fucks," the bigger one said.

"Ten-to-one odds, their mommies still wipe their noses," said the other one.

Then the big, good-looking guy looked at me. I concentrated on putting glasses on my tray, but I could feel him staring.

"You're not Tavarelli's kid, are you?" he said. "I thought your hair was shorter."

My cheeks were burning, and I wanted to cry, but all I could do was look him in the eyes and say, "It's a wig."

He smiled, but not like he was laughing at me. I liked him better already.

"I love a girl who's honest," he said. "Aren't enough to go around."

He curled his finger at me with one hand and reached into his pocket with the other. When I got close, he slid his hand onto the back of my neck.

"Almost feels real," he said.

My heart was pounding, and not all from fear. I liked the hint of garlic on his breath, and the smell of Brut cologne on his cheek as he leaned close to my face. I knew the smell because one of my short-lived boyfriends used to wear Brut, except on him it was stupid because he was barely old enough to shave. But on this guy . . . I felt the crispness of a new bill against my hand and peeked down to see that it was a fifty he was giving me. Then he let go and leaned back against the bar, smiling at me. I felt like melting.

As I picked up the tray of sodas for the boys in the back, the big guy said, "Tell them to remember to clean behind their ears."

I looked, and smiled.

"What's your name?" he asked.

"Catherine," I said, blushing even more.

"Mine's Joey. Joey Valentino."

I had to lean against the bar for a second when he said that. Joey Valentino was a big name in this neighborhood. He was a wannabe who'd actually made it. At least that's what people said.

Joey was tan, with a strip of paler skin over his ears and on his neck, showing off a new haircut. Word was that as a kid, he used to do small stuff for Mario. Suddenly, when he was eighteen, he took off for California. People say it practically broke Mario's heart. No one knew what Joey did in L.A., or why he came back, but for Mario it was like he never left. It was obvious a lot of Mario's heavies were jealous of Little Italy's prodigal son, but they wouldn't dare complain too loudly.

"Oh yeah, I almost forgot," Joey said. "Tell

your brother Mickey that I like how he did today. He can come see me any time he wants
more work."

The tray shook in my hands. I couldn't wait
for the night to be over.

Chapter Three

Gatto's closed early, and I was home before midnight. Pop and Mickey were at the kitchen table. The cigarette smoke was so thick, the flowers on the already stained wallpaper seemed to be wilting. Since Pop was in the middle of a story, they hardly noticed me as I pushed past Mickey's chair to the refrigerator.

I was glad I was wearing one of Mickey's old Yankees hats, so they couldn't see the matted mess the wig had made of my hair. Grabbing some cold cuts, I almost dropped the mayonnaise bottle because someone hadn't screwed the cap on all the way. All that was left of the loaf of bread on the counter were two ends. Ma must've worked late. God forbid Pop or Mickey should walk half a block to the store.

Especially when Mickey was "working" now. I gritted my teeth, saving my anger for later, when I could confront Mickey alone. Little sister or not, I was going to kill him if he was playing gangster instead of going to college. What the hell was Ma working overtime at Macy's for anyway? What the fuck was I busting my feet for at Gatto's? I mean, glamour was great at the start of my shift, but by the end I couldn't help remembering that McDonald's or Grand Union also couldn't cover a college education, whereas Gatto's might. Angry, I spread the mayonnaise so hard, the knife broke through the bread.

"There was four guys," Pop was saying in his contrived tough-guy voice, "and your uncle Vinnie and I couldn't see no way out."

Rolling my eyes, I ground my teeth harder together and put American cheese on the bread.

"Didja kill 'em, Pop?" Mickey said.

I heard the chair scrape the floor as he pulled closer.

"Nah. They was Mario's guys, you know? I wanted Mario to know I wasn't scared. I figured when he heard I was a stand-up guy, he'd have some work for me. Them guys weren't gettin' nothin' outta me, or your uncle Vinnie." Pop leaned back in his chair and lit another cigarette. He sipped some of Mickey's Southern Comfort from the bottle.

I bit into my sandwich, trying to keep quiet. If Ma'd been awake, she'd have smacked Pop in the head. But then, he might have smacked back. I couldn't afford a bruise—I had to work the next day.

Pop continued. "See, I knew those guys

15

weren't from the Bandalinis. I knew they was Mario's. It was a test."

Mickey swigged from the bottle. "What happened?"

"What happened is I got this . . . ." Pop pushed up the sleeve of his checkered robe. There was a thick white scar on his forearm. He clenched his fist to make it stand out.

I couldn't take it. "Mickey, why do you listen to this bullshit?" I yelled. "You know what Ma said. He got that stupid scar from slicing bacon here, in this kitchen!"

Mickey glared at me.

"Your mother don't know everything!" Pop whispered harshly. "And keep your voice down, little miss. Your mother's sleeping."

Biting into my sandwich again, I chewed hard.

"Them guys took your uncle Vinnie and me to the shipping yard, over there, 'cross the river. In Brooklyn . . ."

Last month, it had been, "They tied your uncle Vinnie up and took me to the tenements on Avenue D." Another time, there had been six wiseguys and no Uncle Vinnie. It always ended the same way . . .

"Mario clapped me on the back, and—"

"Pop, would you cut it out?" I said, sputtering pieces of sandwich onto the table. "Just leave Mickey alone. He don't need to hear stupid stories . . ." I started to sound like a New Yorker when I got mad. Grabbing the Southern Comfort, I said, "I swear, you're driving me to drink!"

Pop grabbed my hand. For a bony old drunk, he still had a good grip. "You're seventeen. We don't drink at seventeen in this house."

"Mickey's drinking!"

"Mickey is eighteen. Also, it is his bottle. Also, he doesn't yap like you do. Be quiet, little girl."

It looked like Pop was going to say more, or slap me, or something, but then he sagged. He gave me that hound-dog look that always made me want to hug him.

Pop pushed back his chair, took one last swallow of Southern Comfort and shuffled down the hall toward his bedroom. He forgot his slippers under the kitchen table, and I thought, His feet will get cold. I hurried upstairs to my bedroom.

In my room, I started counting the money I'd made. It had been busy that night, and there were a lot of bills spread out on my bed to sort. I felt slighted, thinking how much I could've made if Mario hadn't closed early for no reason.

I shouldn't say that—Mario always had his reasons.

I liked to keep my money neat. Each bill was flattened between my hands, then placed faceup in a stack according to denomination. When I heard a knock from the bathroom, which separated Mickey's room from mine, I shoved the unsorted bills under my pillow.

I unlocked the door, and Mickey came in, wearing the hound-dog look he learned from Pop. He ruffled my hair. Free of the baseball cap, chestnut-colored tufts poked out of the front and back, where the rubber bands had been.

"Is that the new style uptown?" Mickey said.

He thought I waitressed in a cafe on the Upper West Side.

I shrugged, like I didn't know my hair was a mess. "Must be from wearing that hat all the way home."

Mickey sat on the edge of my bed. "You shouldn't talk to Pop like that. He's not a bad guy."

"That's my point!" I said. "He's *not* a bad guy, or a wiseguy, or anything but a garbageman!"

"He *did* work for Mario."

"As a *garbageman!*"

"Can you prove commercial garbage is a legitimate business? Can you prove Mario's mob dealings don't mix with his business?" Mickey pulled a cigarette from the pack he kept rolled in his sleeve. "Mind if I smoke?"

"Not if you give me one," I said, even though I had a pack in my purse. I didn't want Mickey to know I smoked a pack a day.

He snorted but gave me the cigarette. Emptying pennies out of a jar, I put it on the floor between us for an ashtray.

I ran my hand over Mickey's curly black hair. Even though he was a year older than me, I had always been his protector. When he got in fights at school, I could never stand to watch him get the shit beat out of his pretty round face. So I'd jump in, kicking shins, pulling hair and biting. Fighting "like a girl" always seemed like the best way to win a fight. When the guys fought "clean," both sides limped away bleeding.

Mickey used to scream at me for breaking up his fights. Said he'd never make it in this neighborhood if his sister always fought his battles. That's what I was hoping for. I was waiting for the day he'd get out. I thought then he could become a real big brother and take care of me. When he was accepted at Hunter College, I thought for sure he was making his break.

"So, what'd you do today?" I said, hoping that if he had to lie, it would be good enough to fool me.

His neck got shorter as his shoulders tensed. He smoked faster.

"How was school?" I asked. "What classes did you have today?"

Mickey and I were too close for him not to notice, by my tone, that I knew something. He was probably wondering what I knew, and how I'd heard, so he could prepare the best answer.

"Well, you know," he said, blowing smoke through his nose. "School's 'bout the same."

There were three times when Mickey talked dumb—when he was with his dumber friends, when he was making moves on a girl, and when he was lying.

"Joey Valentino says he might have some work for you. Some *more* work," I said.

"Hey, Sis, why doncha get offa my back?" Mickey said. "School's no big thing. You always said I was so smart. I could do it with my eyes closed, and with a hangover too. I ain't a baby. I can do a little work on the side. Hell, *you* do, and you're still in high school, and another thing, I don't want you talking to Joey Valentino no more. He's not the type you should be hanging around."

I tried to keep from yelling, so we wouldn't wake Ma and Pop. "*You* obviously hang around Joey Valentino's type!"

"That's different," Mickey said. "*I* can handle it. Anyway, the pay's good."

"Oh yeah, like you used to handle those fights in junior high."

Mickey shook a finger in my face. "I never told you I needed help. I told you to stay outta it! Fuck it, if it weren't for you, I mighta been able to work in this neighborhood sooner!"

"Whatcha doin' for Joey?" I asked. I was glad that I'd impeded Mickey's delinquency for a while, and pissed that I hadn't been as successful lately.

Mickey shrugged and got out two more cigarettes. He lit mine for me. "Nothin' like you're thinking," he said.

"What am I thinking?"

"All I'm saying is that I didn't do anything that could get me in trouble."

"Why not?" I said, going to the window. The room was filling with smoke. "Isn't that what you want? Trouble? Otherwise, you could get a job at the Grand Union."

Mickey moved next to the window with me. He looked older than I liked. "Trouble pays good," he said, calmly, no longer using his

21

gangster voice. "Staying out of trouble never did much good for this family. If Poppy Joe hadn't left us this apartment, we wouldn't have a pot to piss in."

"So, you want to be like Poppy Joe," I said. "You want to go to jail? Maybe you just want to die young."

Mickey rolled his eyes and started to leave. "All I'm saying is if everyone did things your way, we'd be sharing a bedroom in a rathole. Poppy Joe might not have been all that great, but he left us with a decent place to live!"

"You're not even Sicilian!" I said. "You'll never be more than an errand boy!"

"I'm worth something!" he said, and slammed the bathroom door. A second later, the door to his room slammed shut.

Tossing my cigarette out the window, I marched through the bathroom and knocked on Mickey's door. He swung it open and glared at me.

"I better not find out you're not going to school," I said. As I stomped back to my room, I said over my shoulder, "I'll tell Ma, you know. Don't think you're too old for a beating."

Chapter Four

I lay in bed that night like I did most nights—
stiff like a board, lonely and scared. I missed the
time before Poppy Joe died, when we lived in a
little apartment two blocks closer to Canal
Street and a block over, on Mott. It was more
Chinatown than Little Italy, and that suited me
fine.

Mickey and I shared a room in the old apartment. Sometimes I'd read to him at night. One
of his favorite books was *James at Fifteen,* which
I reread five times when I was eight and Mickey
was nine. I would sneak a lamp under my covers
to see by, and Mickey would keep an ear cocked
to warn me if Ma and Pop were coming to
check on us.

When Mickey finally fell asleep, I would lie
awake and listen to his breathing. I would tell
him what I was thinking—what guy I thought
was cute at school, what girls I hated for being
stuck-up. I would tell him, while he slept, my
Pierce Brosnan fantasies, where I would be in a
real-life episode of *Remington Steele,* and Pierce
would rescue me.

Eventually, Mickey's even breaths and light

snores would put me to sleep. If I woke up scared during the night, I could take my blanket and pillow and sleep on the floor next to Mickey's bed.

I wasn't scared of monsters, then or now. Monsters would be a relief. I was scared of sleep. What if I fell asleep and didn't wake up? What if I stopped breathing in my sleep?

I could feel my fingers and toes clenching and consciously tried to make them relax. My jaw hurt from grinding my teeth. A sudden twinge in my chest made me want to run to Mickey's room, but we were too old for that now. Still, I thought, I would rather die of a heart attack with someone near. Please, I thought, I don't want to die alone. Just let me live one more night!

Rolling onto my stomach made my chest feel better, but it was harder to breathe. The pillow kept covering half my face. Just when I thought I'd gotten the right position, my ankle started to itch. Scratching it with my other foot, I noticed an itch on my back. As I scratched that, another itch appeared on my stomach. Then behind my knee. By this time, my neck was hurting from trying to stay in a comfortable position on the pillow while scratching.

I rolled onto my side, but my arm started to

fall asleep from being crushed under my body, so I rolled onto my back again. I wished for Mickey's gentle snore to lull me to sleep, or at least his bottle of Southern Comfort.

I began to count backward from a hundred. With each number, I made tight fists. Sometimes this worked to put me to sleep. By the time I got to fifty my hands would stop clenching, by thirty my counting would get confused, and I would be asleep before getting down to twenty.

I counted down to one and was still very awake, although my hands and forearms were tired from making fists. The bed felt hard against my butt. Realizing that my eyes were scrunched painfully closed, I willed my face to relax. My sense of dread had become a fire at the base of my skull, burning up into my brain and down my spine.

Sitting up in bed, I felt the floor for my purse. I finally located the strap, poking out from under the bed. The purse was full of un-counted bills, which arguing with Mickey had kept me from putting away. After a while, I found a box of Marlboro Lights under the money and bits of rubbish. There were only two cigarettes left. I lit one.

Staring at my digital clock, I willed the numbers—2:05—to blur. I thought it might make me sleepy. Sucking smoke, I kept staring until the clock said 2:08. I smelled something funny and jerked out of my trance in time to notice that the long ember from my cigarette had fallen onto the bed. As I patted the ashes, which had barely singed the sheets, I wondered why I wasn't surprised that I might have gone up in flames if I'd succeeded in willing myself to sleep. I expected disaster. Sometimes, I thought I even *wanted* it. Then someone would take care of *me* for a change. Anyway, it didn't matter whether I was *afraid* to die in my sleep or if I wanted it. Either way, I lay awake half the night.

Pulling a robe on, I tiptoed downstairs without turning on the light. I stepped over the fifth step down because it creaked. I instinctively avoided tripping over Pop's work shoes outside the kitchen. By the time I got to the cabinet over the sink, my eyes had adjusted to the dark, so I didn't have to risk knocking over a glass by accident. I got one of the highballs, filled it quietly with Southern Comfort at the table, and retraced my steps to my room.

Sitting by the window, I sipped the drink

and savored the glow in my throat, chest and stomach. I lit my last cigarette, this time flicking ashes out the window. Listening to the cars honking to each other all around me was nice. Some of those cars were probably on their way out of Manhattan right now. Maybe to Long Island, or Connecticut. I pictured a station wagon with a mom and dad in the front seat, talking about Cousin Billy's new girlfriend and Grandma's cataracts. In the backseat, two kids, Jody and Ralph, are fighting about sleeping space. Finally they fall asleep with Ralph's head on the floor and his feet up over the top of the seat. Jody is scrunched into a tight ball. Neither of them realizes that if one had climbed over the seat, way into the back, then both of them could've spread out. They'd rather be together, even if it's uncomfortable.

Chapter Five

My friend Erica from next door waited for me outside our buildings before school. Yelling good-bye to Ma and Mickey, who was rubbing Ma's neck at the kitchen table, I hurried outside. A group of girls on their way to St. Patrick's School chattered past Erica on the sidewalk, like she wasn't there.

It was interesting to me that an Asian girl was giggling with a white girl. In our school that wouldn't happen—the Italians, blacks and Asians kept their own cliques. The only mixing was among the nerds, the jocks—whose clique was the team—and the artists, who were too busy outdoing everybody else in weirdness to be racist.

"Bitches," Erica said quietly about the St. Patrick's girls, so only I could hear.

She shoved her hands into the pockets of her leather biker jacket. She wore motorcycle boots over tight Levi's, and a leather thong around her neck, with the Harley emblem dangling from it. Soon, she always bragged, she would have enough money to buy a bike, and then watch out, New York! It didn't matter that she only had a thousand in the bank and that it was supposed to pay for college next year. "I'm just waiting for my father to die," she'd say. "I expect to invite you to the funeral any month now."

"How do you know they're bitches?" I argued, staring after the Catholics.

Erica shrugged. Not having any religion, she wouldn't understand if I told her I used to wish I could go to St. Patrick's. Theoretically, I was Catholic. But other than for Poppy Joe's funeral, and midnight Mass on Christmas, I hadn't been to church with my family since I was ten. When Mickey and I became adolescents, Ma and Pop got too busy to bother with church. I guess they didn't figure it was doing them any good anyway, since they still weren't any nearer to being able to afford a future. I think the final straw for Ma was when she realized that she was never going to leave the neighborhood and get a house on Long Island, or even in Queens.

Erica interrupted my thoughts. "So tell me everything about your weekend," she said, punching me in the arm.

"I worked Friday and Saturday," I said.

"That's what I *mean*," she said. "What happened at work? Anything good? What was your biggest tip? Any cute wiseguys try to hit on you? Any fights? Did you find out about getting me some you-know-what?"

I smiled, mostly because the tips *had* been good. Otherwise, Erica would've annoyed me with all her stupid questions. If she wanted to know so bad, why didn't *she* go to work in a social club? Although that wasn't really fair to say. She would love to work at Gatto's but was afraid she wasn't Italian enough to get a job there. Anyway, Mario didn't need two cocktail waitresses.

I answered, "Nothing. No. Fifty dollars. Sort of. No—and anyway, they wouldn't fight inside the club. No."

Erica stomped her foot. "Like I remember everything I asked you, in order! Just tell me everything!"

So I told her about the guy on Friday night who was nice to me, and about Mario talking to me. I didn't mention that the guy was Joey Valentino. I also didn't mention that Mickey's name was brought up twice on Friday, and again on Saturday, because Erica would roll her eyes and tell me to stop becoming my mother.

"What about . . ." and Erica put her finger under her nose and sniffed.

"I already told you," I complained, "I can't go around trying to buy dope where I work! Want me to lose my job?"

I shouldn't have snapped at Erica like that. We both wanted to get some cocaine. We tried it once in the bathroom at a school dance because Erica's then-boyfriend had scored some. It was fun, because suddenly I felt like I could actually dance, and I did, which was a lot better than hiding in the corner, feeling suicidal. It was nice to feel like I belonged for once. I actually got my first boyfriend that night. He was a jerk and only lasted two weeks, but what a great two weeks it was!

Right now, there wasn't a point in even *looking* for drugs. There wasn't anyone I wanted to belong with anyway. I was tired of the little boys, especially after meeting Joey. Erica, however, was relentless.

She shrugged. "It's no big *deal*," she said, like I'd offended her. "I just wanted you to keep your ears open."

"I always do," I said, which was true. I listened to everything and said practically nothing when I was at work. Someday I wanted to be a writer, and I figured if there was one good thing about working for Mario, it was the literary possibilities. Under my mattress I kept a notebook with ten pages already full of observations I'd made at work.

"Uh-oh," Erica said. "Dork alert!"

Frankie was strutting his stuff up ahead, surrounded by his protectors, friends and other hangers-on. They swayed from side to side like one animal. Thick gold chains glittered from their necks in the sunlight. Frankie's chains were the biggest.

"My God," I said, "it's a giant wannabe! Must've escaped from the zoo!"

We giggled, and Erica cooed, "Here, wanna-wanna, here, wannabe, come to Mommy, wannabe, wanna snack, cute little wannabe?"

"You better watch it," I said, jabbing Erica in the ribs. "He might not always be a wannabe, he might actually take Mario's place someday!"

"Bullshit. He's too stupid even for that."

We laughed again and sat on the school steps to share a cigarette before the morning bell. Frankie and his crew sat higher up, at the other end. We ignored them, even after spitballs began to mysteriously appear near us on the cement. I was sure now that Frankie wasn't connecting me with the long-haired waitress from Gatto's.

"Hey," Erica said, cupping a hand over her

eyes against the sun, "isn't that your hunky brother? Man, he's such a babe!"

I looked where she was pointing and saw that it was Mickey. He supposedly had a nine o'clock class this morning, but it didn't look like he intended to go. He'd passed the subway, and he wasn't carrying his books.

"I'll kill him," I said, standing.

A spitball hit me in the ear. Although I grimaced, I didn't bother to respond to Frankie and his crew. I had to hurry, or I'd lose Mickey.

"I have to go," I said. "Maybe I'll see you later."

Then I took off at a trot after Mickey. I half expected Erica to follow me, especially since that day was a gym day, which she hated anyway. But her father would get out the belt if he found out she cut school again, while my father probably wouldn't even notice.

Chapter Six

I caught up with Mickey as he ducked onto Bowery. Slowing down, I hung back so he wouldn't see me. A guy in a wheelchair shook a coffee cup at me. What nerve! He lived four blocks away from me with two hookers and another deadbeat—on my way home from school, I usually saw him on his way home, *walking* his wheelchair.

Weaving in between delivery trucks to keep hidden, I followed as Mickey turned on Houston and returned to Mulberry Street, heading back toward the neighborhood. Like brother, like sister—I wondered if he ever followed me to work and had only been pretending to go along with my lies for the past month.

Pretty soon Mickey ended up on a stoop a block from our building. Although it was barely nine in the morning, his friends already had a card game going. I watched from behind a tan Buick as they dealt him in. Knowing I couldn't stay there forever, I hoped if Mickey was going to get into trouble, he would do it soon. Not that skipping school wasn't trouble enough. It would be, if Ma ever found out.

My legs tingled from the strain of crouching, and I knew a major cramp was coming. As sweat trickled down my back and my jeans started to feel heavy, I wished even more for one of the St. Patrick's School kilts. In my school, wearing a skirt only meant it was easier for lamebrains like Frankie to peek at your underwear, or even pull it down. And a skirt made it harder to catch them afterward, though I guessed that a skirt might make kicking them in the balls easier than tight jeans—more swing in the leg. Not that anyone would ever kick Frankie in the balls. His mother would come after you with a broomstick, and she wasn't afraid to use it!

Someone was stopping at the stoop. A tall guy with a dark blue suit—Italian and double-breasted, of course—bent and spoke to Mickey. The guy had his tie loosened and his shirt open a few buttons. Even so, he must be sweating. He looked familiar, so I figured I must've seen him at Gatto's sometime.

Then I realized he was the cute guy from Friday night—Joey Valentino, the perfect image of a coming-of-age mobster, straight out of Universal Studios. My brain must be frying, I thought, how come I didn't recognize him right off? Wishful thinking, I guess. I'd hoped it was just someone asking for directions or something.

Mickey got off the stoop, against the loud protests of his friends. Joey reached into his pocket and tossed a coin at them. Man oh man, I bet their faces were red! Probably he told them to call someone who cared. They were lucky he felt like joking and didn't just kick someone in the mouth. His reputation was why Mickey didn't want *me* hanging around Joey, even though he couldn't understand why I felt the same way about *him* and Joey.

For an instant I thought I saw Joey smile in my direction as he walked down the street with Mickey. But he couldn't have seen me. Pretty soon Joey got into a car, and Mickey continued on his own. Although I hated being on the same side of the street as our building, it was the only way to keep Mickey from seeing me. I hoped none of the old ladies would call out to me. Whichever side of the street I was on, I was probably screwed—it was pretty good odds that one of the ladies would tell Ma I hadn't been in school today. They'd pretend they weren't really tattling—"Your daughter was acting funny today, sneaking around the neighborhood, hiding behind cars. I said to Loretta, what's wrong with the Tavarelli girl? She sick?"

Mickey turned onto Kenmare, walked two blocks and went into the deli on the corner of Broadway. When he returned with a bag, I jumped out of my hiding place and ran across the street to confront him.

"Catherine!" he said. "Why the fuck ain't you in school?"

"Why the fuck ain't *you* in school?" I said, mimicking him. Grabbing the bag from his hands, I said, "And who do you think you are, running errands for Joey Valentino? You his little errand boy now? Or just his dope courier!"

"Who says Joey deals?" Mickey said, reaching for the bag.

I backed up. "I'm not giving it to you until you tell me the truth, Mickey. What are you carrying around the city for Joey?"

"It's his fucking *lunch,* you happy?" Mickey said, grabbing at me again.

"Uh-uh," I said. "Too big. Too heavy."

"And a carton of cigarettes," Mickey said. "Why don't you just look inside?"

"Right *here*?" I said. "Don't you think it'll look a little suspicious? What if there're cops around? What if they've been following you?"

I was only half joking. If there were drugs in the bag, Mickey and I could both go to jail, or both end up dead, which I wished I'd thought of before taking the bag away from Mickey. While I was thinking, Mickey grabbed my arm and ripped the bag away from me. I clutched the piece of brown paper still in my fist while Mickey shoved the open bag in my face. It smelled like pastrami. The hard corner of a carton of Marlboro reds almost poked my eye out. Boy, did I feel stupid. Now I couldn't even yell at him for skipping school, since I'd skipped out too.

I considered asking Mickey if he wanted to do something together after he dropped off Joey's lunch. Instead, I turned away with my chin in the air and said, "Better not *ever* let me catch you delivering dope for Joey Valentino!"

I was trying too hard not to cry to hear what Mickey said as I stomped away. I hoped Erica had some extra late passes in her locker.

Chapter Seven

So I yell after Catherine, "And I better not catch you following me again!" But she doesn't even answer me, she just keeps walking.

So I'm like, she better be going back to school now. My sister's really crafty sometimes, and as I'm heading over to Mario's place on Mott Street, I'm thinking, it would be just like Cat to hide someplace and then start following me around again, like she's my mother or something. Fuck it, I think. I'll follow *her* back to the school.

I'm having trouble finding her, so I'm thinking she's probably behind me, and I pretend to tie my shoe, then I look between my legs to see if she's there. All I see is Mrs. Cortese swatting my buddy Mike on the back of his legs with a broom, chasing him inside their house. Oh man, are the guys gonna laugh when I tell 'em.

I get to the school and see Catherine stomping up the front steps. For a second I feel like I should yell out or something, because I don't mean to disappoint her, but maybe she shouldn't be so hard to please. Anyway, I have my own fucking problems, and now I'm late getting Joey his lunch.

As I head back toward Mario's social club, I try to walk like a wiseguy. I know the guys are checking me out from the stoop when I pass, and I raise my hand but don't really wave, because Joey sent *me* on an errand, twice in one week, no shit! So now I have an image to protect. As I pass by, I see Tony picking his nose and wiping the snot on the stoop railing. Shit, I hope Joey has some more work—some *real* work for me soon, because I don't fucking want to be hanging around stoop losers all my fucking life.

Catherine thinks she's so great because she wants out of this neighborhood, and I'm like, so the fuck what—don't we all? Thing is, it's easy for her—she's smart, and she wants to be a writer, and to go to college. I don't like to write, I don't even like to read, so like why do I have to go to college? It's fucking stupid. I just want to make some good money and move away from here. Someplace warm, like maybe Florida or California.

I knock on the tinted glass door of Mario's club and hope I'll be invited in, but someone just opens it a crack.

"This is for Joey Valentino," I say to the

fat man when he takes the bag from my hands.

As I'm trying to peek around him into the club, he puts a pudgy hand in front of my face. I wonder how much the big gold pinky ring, full of diamonds, cost.

I get a glimpse of the inside before the door shuts. There must've been a party or something, because there were paper streamers hanging from the ceiling and fallen on the floor. Sparkly shit decorated the bar.

Damn! I think, pausing at the curb and looking back. It's just like in the beginning of *Scarface,* the original, black-and-white version, just before the big boss, Louie Costillo, gets whacked. He's like on the phone after a big party, and all you see is Scarface's shadow approaching, whistling a tune. Then he says, "Hiya, Louie," and *pow*! Louie's dead.

As I look back at Mario's, I see a shadow passing behind the dark window, and I'm thinking, Holy shit! Except there's no whistling, just a car honking. I didn't even realize I was standing in the street. Giving the finger to the asshole who's edging his cheap, piece-of-shit car at me, I strut back to the sidewalk.

I'm almost to the corner when the fat man yells at me from Mario's.

41

"Kid! Joey wants to see you!"

I run back and accidentally stomp on Fatty's foot at the door. For a second I'm frozen, but then he stops glaring and laughs, so now I'm red and embarrassed. Fuckin' A!

Joey's eating his sandwich at the bar, and I sit next to him. He shoves a beer over to me, and I try real hard to swallow past the lump in my throat. Since he's busy chewing, I'm pretty sure I didn't fuck up with his lunch, like by getting mayonnaise instead of mustard or something.

When he smiles at me, I feel pretty good, so I swig some more beer and say, "You were living in California, right? I'm thinking of moving there. How was it?"

Then, because I still want to work for him, I add, "Is there lots of, you know, work out there? How does a guy go about, you know, finding the right employment?"

I could swear he said, "Do it first, do it yourself, and keep on doin' it," just like Scarface said in the movie.

So I nod.

I'm real confused when Joey goes, "Great. The broom's in the kitchen."

I just stare, because I don't know what he means.

"Whatsa matter?" he says. Then he pats my

back and smiles. "Sorry, I forgot you probably want to be paid in advance. Smart."

Pulling two twenties from his jacket pocket, he folds them into my hand and says, "You can finish your beer first. Just make sure this place is clean before five. If Mario finds one sparkle on the floor, he'll know someone besides Paulie cleaned up, and we wouldn't want Paulie to get into trouble."

I nod again and, sipping my beer one more time, I go to get the broom. Joey gets up, wipes his mouth with a hanky and gestures to Paulie and the fat man by the door.

"We'll be back in an hour. I'm locking the door, and you keep it that way, okay?" Joey says as the fat wiseguy opens the door for him.

Joey's so cool. He's totally like the prodigal son they taught at catechism, or more like it, catastrophic school. You know, the guy comes back and *makes* it. *Big-time.*

When they leave, I finish my beer quickly. At first I was embarrassed that all Joey wanted me for was a cleaning boy, but now I remember how in *Goodfellas* the kid started just by parking cars. It takes a while for them to know they can trust you with the big stuff. I'll show them.

Holding my head high while I sweep up confetti and streamers, I'm like picturing the fat man's diamond pinky ring on my little finger. There's a scar under my eye from a knife fight with three young wiseguys from Brooklyn who tried to move in on my boss's territory.

Real loud, I say to the walls, "I don't see nothin' and I don't hear nothin', and when I do, I don't tell the cops."

Just like *Scarface.*

Chapter Eight

I ignored Mickey for a few days. Even though I sometimes threatened, I wasn't a tattletale, and I didn't tell Ma that Mickey wasn't going to school. So I was surprised on Thursday, when I came home from studying at Erica's house and heard Ma screaming from the living room.

The curls in Ma's thick black hair had frizzed out, like always happened when she was mad. It looked worse than usual, so she must have been tugging at it for hours. That was how she worked herself up for confrontation, like a cat whose hair stands on end.

Mickey sat in the corner of the couch, trying to look cool, but I could tell he was scared. He was wearing shorts, and his sweaty skin was probably stuck now to the plastic slipcover. With his eyes fixed on the heeled shoe Ma was shaking at him, he was probably wondering if he could get unstuck quick enough to escape a blow.

But Ma didn't use the shoe. She collapsed on the other end of the couch and started to cry. It made me want to pick up the shoe myself and hit my brother.

"Why would you do this to me?" she said. "Do you hate me so much?"

"Aw, Ma, why do you have to take everything so personally? It's about *me,* not you."

"Is it wrong for me to want my children to have an education? What do you want to do with your life? You want to get married, have kids . . ."

"Ma, I don't even have a girlfriend."

Ma waved at him to shut up. "You want to be a garbageman when you grow up?"

"I *am* grown up, Ma." Now Mickey started to yell. "Why can't you just let me run my own life?"

"Whose house is this? Yours?" Ma said. "Why am I working fifty, sometimes sixty hours a week in goddamn Macy's Housewares? And what about the money I gave you for your first semester? Gone?"

Mickey sighed. "I still got everything but the registration fee. I was saving it for you. I'm not a thief," he said through clenched teeth, like he was offended she should bring up her own money with him.

Mickey moved on the couch, and I could hear the suction as his legs ripped free of the plastic. Ouch, I thought. He lit a cigarette.

"Get an ashtray," Ma said.

I ducked behind the stairs so Mickey wouldn't see me. I wanted to hear the end of this. If they knew I was there, they'd send me to my room.

"If you're so smart," Ma yelled, "how come you didn't answer me? What are you going to do with your life? How do you think you can earn a living without a college education?"

Mickey came back with the ashtray, and I slipped out of my hiding place. I saw Ma pull two tissues from her purse, one for her eyes and one to slide under the ashtray Mickey had placed on the glass coffee table. I wondered why they were even having this conversation in the living room, which was supposed to be only for company and special occasions.

"I'll go back to college eventually, Ma. I just don't know what I want to do yet."

"That's what college is for, to figure that out!" Ma said, taking one of Mickey's cigarettes for herself. She coughed. She wasn't supposed to be smoking because of her heart, but at least she wasn't crying anymore.

"I won't go," Mickey said.

"You're not living in this house, where everyone is working, even your little sister, and growing into a bum."

"I have a job, Ma."

47

Although I couldn't see her face, I pictured Ma's eyes widening as much as my own.

"Where?" she said. "For how long? Where's this money you're making? You don't think you have to contribute to this family too?"

Mickey took out his wallet and placed a small stack of bills on the table. "I'm working, you know, around. Odd jobs, errands, stuff like that. So there's not much there, but Joey Valentino says—"

"Oh no," Ma said, standing. She picked up the bills and tossed them in Mickey's face. Coughing again, she shrieked, "You tell Mr. Valentino to shove his job up his well-groomed asshole!"

Go, Ma! I thought.

"Forget it, I'll tell him myself. I'll find him, and—"

"Don't you dare, Ma!" Mickey said, standing and facing her. He was taller than her by two inches, at least, and his muscles stood out on his arms, but Ma didn't flinch.

Staring back at him, she said, "You sit," and pointed at the couch.

As Mickey sat, I stepped back under the stairs again because Ma was heading my way. She looked like a soldier as she stomped into the kitchen, and I cringed, because I knew what was coming. A kitchen drawer slid open, and its insides crashed to the floor. Then Ma came back, carrying the wooden spoon that had never been used for mixing.

"Bend over," Ma said.

"Ma! I'm eighteen years old! You can't—"

"You going to live in my house? You going to talk back to me? Then you will feel what I can do."

I heard Mickey sobbing before I heard the first *whack!* of the spoon. Even though I was proud of Ma for standing up to him, and especially for telling him off about Joey Valentino, I wished she hadn't gotten the spoon. Mickey really *was* too old, and I felt like crying for him. My cheeks felt hot and red with his humiliation. I ran upstairs and slammed my door hard enough for Ma to know how I felt, but not enough to give her a reason to bring the spoon upstairs to me.

A minute later, I heard Mickey stomping angrily to his room, and then I heard Pop come home. Ma started screaming at him right away. Opening my door a crack, I leaned my head against the wall and listened.

"This is what your goddamn fantasies have gotten us!" Ma shouted. "A boy in college? A lawyer, someday, maybe? No."

It made me sick to hear Ma talking like that. For one thing, if it didn't work out with Mickey, maybe *I* could be a lawyer someday. No one ever seemed to think of that angle. Anyway, just because Mickey was running errands for Joey didn't mean he was lost forever. Hell, I worked at Gatto's, and I was okay. But they didn't know about that.

"I'll talk to him," Pop said.

"You've done enough talking. You're ruining that boy's life with all your talking."

"I'll tell him the truth," Pop said. As his foot creaked on the fifth step, I closed my listening crack. It didn't matter—they were yelling so loud, Erica could probably hear them next door.

"What do you call the truth?" Ma argued.

"I'll tell him that the mob is serious, and dangerous, and not something to play around with . . ."

"How about the *real* truth?" Ma screamed. "How about telling him that you don't know *anything* about the mob? You've never known *anything*! Tell him that he's becoming the wannabe you always were, and look where it got you!"

I heard Mickey's door shut and knew he'd been listening too. I hated when they argued like he wasn't there. I was about to cut through the bathroom to Mickey's room and see if he was okay when I heard Pop's tired steps continuing up the stairs. I could practically hear him wheezing. Creeping into the bathroom, I listened at the crack under the door.

"She has no right to talk like that, Pop," Mickey said.

"She has a right. She's your mother."

I heard Pop flicking his lighter, and then finally a match being struck instead.

There was silence for a second, until Pop said quietly, "She's right, you know. My life was never as glamorous as I make it out to be. I'm sorry if my stories confused you . . ."

Mickey laughed in a mean way I'd never heard before. "Pop, I'm not that stupid," he said. "I know you never did nothing with the mob. But you were never on the Yankees either, and I still played Little League."

"That's really deep, kid, but this is serious. Tomorrow you go back to college. You're too old to be shitting around the neighborhood like a little hood."

"I ain't going, Pop. Just 'cause you didn't make it don't mean I can't."

Crack!

"That's for talking like a punk," Pop said. "I thought your ma beat some sense into you, but

51

I guess she's not as strong as she used to be. This isn't the fucking movies, kid. Get a life. And get one fast, because your ma doesn't deserve to be down there crying while she cooks your supper."

There was silence for almost a minute. Then, "Don't you ever hit me again," Mickey said.

I bit my lip. Mickey never talked back to Pop. I was the only one who did that, and I could, because I was a girl. It was the code of the neighborhood.

Crack! again, and then, suddenly, scuffling sounds, and muffled grunts. The door from the bathroom to Mickey's room was locked, so I ran out to the hall.

"Ma!" I yelled as I burst into Mickey's room. Pop and Mickey were wrestling and punching on the floor.

"Stop it!" I screamed.

"Get outta here!" Pop said, puffing between words.

I heard Ma coming up the stairs just as Mickey got on top of Pop, pinning him. Jesus fucking Christ, I thought, he's going to punch him!

"Mickey," I yelled, "don't you dare! You'll kill him! Mickey!"

Now Ma was in the room. She stepped right

into the scuffle and grabbed Mickey's raised arm. It looked like she was going to bite it if he didn't let up.

"Catherine, call the cops," she said, barely moving her mouth.

Mickey's body went slack, and Pop said, "It's okay. It's over." His lip was bleeding, and Mickey had a scratch over his eye.

Ma held Pop's skinny, wasted body against hers and guided him downstairs. I was so mad, I couldn't even cry. My fists were clenched so hard, I could feel my nails making half-moons in my palms.

"I'll kill him if he tries that again," Mickey said. "Fucking bastard. Who the fuck does he think he's talking to? I won't even have to kill him, I'll get someone else—"

"Shut up!" I yelled. "And grow up!"

Mickey just looked at me for a second. His eyes were cloudy, and I felt like he was trying to hate me. I'd betrayed him by standing up for Ma and Pop.

"Get the fuck outta my room," he said.

"Yeah, fine," I said, clenching my fists harder. "Why don't you go watch *Goodfellas* again? A few more times, and maybe you'll know *all* the lines by heart."

Chapter Nine

I didn't speak to Mickey again for the rest of that week, or the next. In the mornings he slept late, probably to piss off Ma and Pop. At night I either went to Erica's to hide, or I burrowed under a blanket with a flashlight so I could try to do my homework, in spite of the screaming downstairs. I would've expected Mickey to back down sooner. I almost respected him for holding his own, even if he was being stupid. Pop seemed thinner and drunker than usual.

For the first time, I was thrilled to be going to work on Saturday night. It had rained all day, and while Pop was sleeping and Ma was at work, Mickey and I were both home. I didn't want to fight, so I had to avoid him all day, which isn't easy when you share a bathroom and the house only has one TV.

The rain was only a drizzling spit when I left, but as I stepped off the curb to get a taxi, my foot sank into a wet puddle of sludge. Cursing to myself, I had the driver drop me directly at Gatto's. The hell with being sneaky. No way was I going to walk four blocks out of my way with mud squishing around my toes. Thank God I wasn't wearing my hooker boots.

Mario and Paulie ignored me when I came in, and Joe, as usual, ignored me while I got ready. When I came out of the kitchen, Paulie made me a piña colada. I sat at the bar, sipping and waiting for the Mafia to bumble in, and feeling okay for the first time since the past week when Ma busted Mickey.

Twirling a long curl from the wig around my fingers, I pretended I was Sharon Stone, or maybe Madonna. A conqueror! Powerful! Sexy! I clicked my needle-sharp heels together.

Before I could finish my drink, a group of guys as dumb as Frankie, only older, came into the club. Sliding off my stool, I pulled my short skirt straight and got ready to take orders.

"It's okay, sweetie, we're sitting at the bar," said a guy with a crooked nose.

"Hey, Paulie! What's doin'?" said another musclebound greaseball.

As they sank onto barstools, Crooked Nose dropped his arm across my shoulders. I smiled. Part of my job was making Mario's customers happy, even when they were jerks. All I could hope was that it would get busy real fast so I could go back to serving drinks. Sometimes entertaining jerks was good for tips, but these guys smelled like bums. What they didn't spend on drinking probably went to pay the two "bodyguards" who were looming over them.

"Have a drink with us," said Crooked Nose. "Paulie, the lady can rest for a bit, can't she? Bring her whatever she likes."

While Paulie made me a fresh piña colada, Crooked Nose squeezed me between him and his friend. Neither offered me his stool.

The other greaseball leaned on the bar and swung his head toward me. He stank like stale rum.

"Call me Howie," he said.

"And I'm Johnny, but you could call me Tiger," said Crooked Nose.

Charmed, I thought. "Catherine," I said, limply offering my hand.

When I tried to shake Howie's hand, he took both my hands in his and clutched them to his chest. His shirt, of course, was open. I wanted to puke.

"Be still, my heart," Howie said. I caught Paulie rolling his eyes as he wiped glasses dry.

"Got a cigarette, Catherine?" said Tiger John.

Leaning forward against the bar, I took a big gulp out of my piña colada. This was too pathetic. Before I could ask Paulie for my purse, he was tossing a half-finished pack of Lucky Strikes onto the bar. He kept them there for bums like these.

"This all you got?" said Howie as he took a cigarette from the pack. "No Marlboro?"

Paulie just glared.

Laughing nervously, Tiger John said, "Just kidding, Paulie. 'Preciate the smokes." Turning to me, he said, "Just got a new car today. A flaming red fucking awesome Corvette. You like cars?"

"I guess," I said.

"After you're done working, we could take you for a ride. Baby, does she cook after dark! I bet she could do ninety, easy, on the Henry Hudson after the traffic dies out for the night. Why don't you come outside and see it? Come on!"

The beefy guy standing behind Tiger's stool moved to the side. His face didn't change, and he kept his hands folded neatly in front of his crotch. You could always tell the wannabes by the size of their bodyguards. And by the lack of subtlety. I mean, Mario was the closest thing to a Godfather around here, but did you see two big lugs standing over him when he drank? Of course not. Mario kept a little guy—little compared to Howie and Tiger's musclemen—standing in the corner, so quiet most people didn't even notice he was there. I saw him move once, when there was a bar fight near Mario's table. Actually, I saw him *after* he moved. He was so fast, it was like the two guys fighting had tossed themselves against the wall.

It was like with talking. The wannabes talked constantly about this score, that hit, and about their love affairs, their cars, their big guns. Mario, on the other hand, barely said ten words a night. But you heard every word he said, and you remembered it. He didn't wanna be, he *was*. Someday I hoped I'd be like him. Not a mobster, but something, anything, that would let me just *be*.

"I can't leave the bar when I'm working," I said to Tiger. "I'm sure it's an awesome car. Maybe another time."

Howie started to tell me about the time when he beat the shit out of a homeless guy with a bat. I leaned my chin against my hand and sank against the bar. Thank God it was almost time for me to fetch Mario's dinner from the kitchen.

I was sucking an ice cube from the bottom of my glass when Tiger yelled, "Fuckin' A!"

He ran outside. Through the tinted glass I could barely see him, but it looked like he was bent over, inspecting what must've been his new car. Then he was jumping up and down. A few seconds later, he was pushing someone in the chest. The someone didn't seem to care.

Meanwhile, Howie was yelling at Tiger's bodyguard. "What the fuck are we paying you for? Get the fuck outside!"

The bodyguard smiled and headed for the door. I headed for the kitchen, where I'd be able to see the action without risking getting caught by a stray bullet or something.

"There's my girl! Where you going, sweetheart?" I heard as I got to the end of the bar.

It was Joey Valentino. He was the "someone" Tiger had been pushing outside. I had to smile. It was worth the risk to lean against the bar and watch as Tiger and his bodyguard came back in. The bodyguard folded his hands over his crotch again and stood by the door. Spit glistening in the corner of his mouth, Tiger put his hand on Joey's shoulder and tried to spin him around. Although Tiger looked strong, Joey didn't move.

"There's a piece of shit on my shoulder. Someone remove it, please," Joey said. He clutched the railing that ran along the bar, like he was trying hard to control himself. But he winked at me at the same time.

His face red and blotchy, Tiger danced around in front of Joey, after first glaring at Howie and the two bodyguards. He glared at me too, while Joey winked at me again. I blushed and climbed onto a barstool. Across the bar, Paulie settled in to watch too, and offered me a cigarette.

"You hit my fucking car, man!" Tiger sputtered.

"You didn't leave me enough space to park," Joey said. I noticed one hand was deep in his jacket pocket.

"Yeah, well, you coulda parked somewhere else," Tiger said to Joey. Then he screamed to the lug, "What the fuck you think you're doin'? Gimme some help over here!"

The big guy started to step forward when Joey shook his head, and the guy shrugged. He stepped back again. Now Tiger was really mad. Howie stared at his drink on the bar.

"This guy hit my fucking car! My brand-fucking-new car! Ain't someone gonna do somethin' about it?"

When no one answered, Tiger pulled his

shoulders back and said, "My father is Sal the Ox . . ."

"The lawyer?" yelled one of Mario's boys.

"Nah," Paulie said, "I think he means the pizza guy down on Broome."

"That true?" Joey said. "Your father makes good pizza?"

Tiger raised his arm, but before his fist reached Joey's nose, he stopped. I couldn't see much from where I was sitting, but Joey's hand wasn't in his pocket anymore. I couldn't tell whether he had a gun against Tiger's gut or just had Tiger's balls in his fist, but either way was bad enough for Tiger.

"Careful, Joey," Paulie said. "This ain't your mother's house."

"Get the fuck out," Joey said to Tiger. He slid his hand back into his pocket.

Then he came to my end of the bar and quietly sat down on the stool next to me. I was amazed that he didn't watch Tiger and his crew run out and drive away. What if Tiger had pulled a gun and shot him in the back? How did he know he wouldn't?

As if reading my mind, Joey said, "Jerk doesn't even have a bat in his car." He smiled, and I blushed.

"The usual, Paulie," he said, getting up. "Have the girl bring it to the table."

By the time I got Joey's drink to him, four other guys had come and sat down at his table. It pissed me off, because I had hoped Joey was going to invite me to sit and drink with him. Even though I already had a good buzz going, it didn't seem like it was going to be busy that night. I felt like getting wasted, so I could keep feeling happy, and maybe sleep well too. Besides, Joey was cute. And anyway, I had to find out what his plans were for Mickey.

"Keyed the driver's side door too," I heard one of the guys say as I brought more drinks. "You shoulda fucked with him longer, Joey. Then I coulda busted the taillights or somethin'."

"What do you think of that?" Joey asked me, twirling a curl of my wig around his finger. I noticed he had very long eyelashes.

I shrugged.

Joey grabbed the guy's face between his forefinger and thumb and said, "How old are you? Fourteen? Next time, you got a beef with a guy, leave his car alone. We're not kids here."

Everyone at the table laughed, even the guy

whose face was still pinched between Joey's fingers. I had a feeling maybe this was for my benefit. When Joey winked at me, I was sure he was playing with me.

It felt good.

Chapter Ten

When I got home, everyone, thank God, was asleep. Before going upstairs, I swiped Pop's spare bottle of whiskey—the one he thought no one knew about—from behind the big can of unused silver polish under the kitchen sink. I had to remember to return it before breakfast in the morning.

With the bottle tucked into the waistband of my jeans and a glass of ice in my hand, I tiptoed to my room. I had a feeling it was going to be a long night. As usual, I wished for my own phone, and for Erica to have her own phone too. She didn't sleep well nights either, so we could stay up talking, instead of me thinking all by myself.

Joey had winked at me at least fifty times as I hustled drinks. I got so distracted, I practically spilled a beer on Mario at one point. With Joey staring at me all the time, I couldn't even concentrate on making money.

Sipping the whiskey, I laid out my tips in neat piles on the floor. I'd made sixty-five dollars, which was pretty good, I guess, for a seventeen-year-old. But usually it was more. That night I hadn't made any "me money," because fifty dollars always went to Ma, and the other fifteen would barely keep me in cigarettes for the week.

The whiskey burned my lips and throat, but it had a sweet aftertaste that I loved. And it would help me sleep. Usually I kept a bottle of blackberry brandy in the closet to gulp from when I couldn't sleep, but it was empty. Monday, maybe Erica would use her fake ID to get me some more.

After putting the night's earnings on top of the dresser, I lay on my belly and reached my arm as far as I could underneath the big antique. There was a manila envelope taped under there, which I pulled out. I patted the dust off my arm and carefully slid a stack of money from the envelope. This was my special stash, my me money, made up of all the extra money I made working at Gatto's, which I wouldn't have made if I was really working in a restaurant uptown or, God forbid, McDonald's. This was where I got the money for my work wig and my hooker boots. It was the money that would eventually buy me a computer so I could write a book about Gatto's.

Sometimes I tried to get started on my book with a pen and notebook, but I never got past making notes and doodling in the margins. I knew a computer was just the kick I needed to create something good and become a real writer, not just someone who lies awake at night, planning literary soirees and making up her own magnificent reviews.

There was two hundred in the envelope. I could probably get the computer I wanted in about three more months, that is, if Joey Valentino kept his sweet blue eyes off me.

As I put the envelope back, I shivered at the thought that popped up in my mind. Refusing to think, I shook my head, lit a cigarette and took a big gulp from my glass of whiskey. The ice had melted, so the booze wasn't as strong as before, but it still burned. My eyes watered.

But it was impossible not to think about Joey. As bad a guy as I figured he probably was, I couldn't help it that his face kept rearing up in my mind, smiling and winking. He looked kind of like Alec Baldwin, only a little darker, a little bigger and with longer eyelashes. My heart was starting to dance around in my chest as I thought about him. When I closed my eyes, I could feel my cheeks getting warm. I'd tried to forget all night, so I could concentrate on my job, but now the night was coming back to me. I started to grin like an idiot as I suddenly remembered that Joey fucking Valentino had asked me to go to dinner with him next Saturday night. It was after his third drink when he said, "I got a table for two every Saturday in my old 'hood. You like seafood?"

I barely choked out a "Yeah."

I'd never had sex before—well, not good sex—but suddenly I had a warm and woolly feeling that made me hope to God he'd ask me, *please!*

Now I remembered that the real reason I almost spilled beer on Mario was that I was so nervous to be asking for the night off. I said yes to Joey Valentino! Mickey would be so jealous! Erica too, but she'd get over it when I told her she was getting the chance to sub for me on Saturday at the club.

I wanted to wake up Mickey and tell him the news, but I couldn't. He should never find out about me and Joey. It wouldn't be good for him—I was supposed to be setting a good example. Everyone knows I'm a nice girl, I thought.

Frowning, I suddenly said to myself, I'm such a fucking idiot. Who the fuck did I think I was, accepting a date with Joey? Is that the crowd I want to hang with? What if he asked me to marry him?

Lighting another cigarette with the butt of the first, I decided it was more important to figure out how I was going to go to dinner with Joey without anyone in my house finding out. And another thing, I thought as I poured another shot of whiskey into my glass, what if Joey's just fucking with my head? What does he really want from me? He's got to be twenty-one or -two years old, and I'm still in high school. He better not fucking be trying to get to Mickey through me. That's probably what Mickey would say, if I asked his opinion.

Now I'm being stupid, I thought. Probably the real reason he wants me is because my breasts are 34C, my waist is thin and my hair, when it's not crumpled from the wig, is soft and nicely curly. Feeling better and smiling to myself again, I thought, And after Saturday, he'll find out that I'm not only cute, I'm a great person. Maybe he'll want me to write a book about him. No, better not tell him I'm going to be a writer. It might make him nervous. He'd be afraid to tell me any secrets.

I rinsed my empty glass in the bathroom sink and filled it with water. After undressing, I climbed into bed naked. The sheets felt cool against my skin, and I wondered what it would feel like to have Joey's leg slung over mine. I wouldn't mind being awake, if I could hear him breathing just inches away from my ear. "Cathy," he'd called me tonight. No one ever called me anything but Catherine or Cat before.

As I worried about whether I'd be able to sleep at all that whole week, my eyelids fluttered shut. The last thing I thought was, I can't wait to tell Erica.

Chapter Eleven

Because I hadn't fallen asleep until four on Sunday night, I had trouble staying awake in English class on Monday. My eyes kept going out of focus when I tried to copy from the blackboard, so I gave up. I could get the notes later from Erica, if she bothered to take any.

I wanted so badly to shut my eyes, but instead I doodled in my notebook to clear my head. I made a puffy heart shape in the middle of a page and shaded it around the edges to look three-dimensional. Adding an arrow cutting through the heart, I carefully drew little feathers at one end, and a realistic point.

I drew another, smaller heart and didn't color it. Inside I wrote, "C.T. Loves J.V."

At the top of the page I wrote slowly, in my best attempt at calligraphy, "Mrs. Catherine Valentino." That was too dumb. I scribbled over it so completely that my pen cut through the paper. Along the margins I wrote "Joey" in different styles—balloon-print, script, fancy calligraphy, tall letters, swirling letters, all capitals.

*A*t our table in the cafeteria, as she split a Hostess cupcake to share with me, Erica said, "So how come you didn't mention Joey Valentino this morning?"

My bologna sandwich suddenly felt thick and dry in my mouth. It wasn't that I wasn't planning to tell Erica, but how did she know? Was it all over the neighborhood? In that case, I was royally fucked.

"What *about* Joey?" I said, picking crumbs off my shirt rather than look Erica in the eye.

"So now it's just 'Joey'? How close are you? Or do you only worship him from afar?" Erica said.

"You have chocolate on your lip," I said.

"Big fucking deal. Are you keeping secrets from me?"

I rolled my eyes. "What'd you hear?" I asked.

Erica rolled her eyes back at me and then reached for my notebook. As she flipped through the pages, she said, "I didn't *hear* anything, I saw *this*." She pointed to a page I'd covered with "Catherine Loves Joey."

I could breathe easier now, even though I was a little embarrassed. At least she hadn't heard a rumor.

"Don't tell anyone," I said. Erica sighed like I was stupid to think she might.

"Joey Valentino asked me out to dinner for Saturday night!" I said.

Screeching, Erica pulled me into a bear hug. Obviously she'd been working out again, because she practically squeezed the breath out of me. "Don't you have to work on Saturday?" she asked.

"Not if you sub for me," I said, and braced myself for another rib-crushing hug.

"Oh my God," Erica said, "what am I going to wear? Do I have to wear heels? I think I'm too tall for that, don't you? Maybe I'll wear that little leather halter top you gave me last Christmas. I guess jeans are out. I wonder if I have a skirt? This is so cool! Hey, maybe Joey will pay you *not* to work anymore! Then I can have your job!"

"Don't forget to keep breathing, you don't want to hyperventilate," I said.

"Yeah, whatever," Erica continued without taking a breath. "Hey, maybe Joey has a friend who'd be interested in me! Someone who rides a Harley, I hope. You think Joey deals coke? Maybe you could get some from him."

Sometimes Erica had a one-track mind. We'd

done cocaine, and now she couldn't wait to get her hands on it again.

"Forget it," I said sternly. "I'm not asking Joey that, and you better not either. Calm down, will you? I'm the one going out on a date with Joey Valentino."

"What are *you* going to wear?" Erica said. "Are you going to wear your wig? Does he even know you wear one?"

"Yeah, he knows, so I'll probably go natural, unless you think I look better in the wig."

Erica shrugged, then shook her head. Thank God, because I didn't want to wear the wig on Saturday. It gave me a headache sometimes, and it was a pain in the ass in the wind. How do people with long hair deal with all that fluff swishing into their eyes all the time?

"So, maybe after your dinner, you and Joey can swing by and see me at work. Maybe we can go out after."

I thought that sounded fun. Then I remembered. "Can't do that," I said. "No women at Mario's place after dark, except whoever's working."

"Maybe you can just come by and pick me up, if you're not doing anything too intimate,"

Erica said, nudging me and winking. "Want to share a bag of pretzels?"

On the way to the snack line, I said, "How are you going to be allowed out so late?"

Erica threw her arm over my shoulder. "I'm sleeping over at your house," she said.

"*I* was planning on sleeping over at *your* house," I said.

"On your first date! Don't you dare. You better make sure he wants you for something more than your body before you stay out all night." Erica shook her finger at me as she scolded. Then she smiled and said sweetly, "That's why you have to pick me up after work. So I can chaperone."

I smacked her on the back of the head. "*Maybe* we'll pick you up, but no promises! I'll give you an extra key to the apartment, in case I'm still out when you finish. Just be sure the lights are all out before you go in. I'm going to pretend I'm working, as usual, and if anyone catches you sneaking into my bedroom, they'll wonder where the fuck *I* am!"

Erica was sucking on a pretzel. When she had gotten all the salt off, she tossed the soggy remains into her empty paper lunch bag. "Just make sure you pick me up. Then you won't have to worry. Remember, I like my men tall and thin. No facial hair, please. At least a high-school education . . ."

Licking the last grains of salt off my own pretzel, I tossed the rest at Erica. "Find your own date!" I said.

"You're gross!" Erica said. "That almost landed in my hair!" With two long, wine-colored fingernails, she picked the wet pretzel off the table where it had landed and tossed it in my lap.

"Gross!" I said, standing up so the pretzel landed on the floor.

"Hey!" Erica said suddenly. "Isn't that your brother? What's he doing with those slobs?"

I looked out the cafeteria window, where she was pointing. It *was* Mickey. He was swaying from side to side, with an extra bounce to his step, like a tough guy. His hair was greased and styled. As I watched, he gave Frankie Wannabe a playful punch in the arm. It was worse than when he hung out with his regular loser friends, I thought. At least they were his age. Kissing up to Frankie was pathetic, even if Frankie might someday have a place in the mob. It was more than pathetic, it was dangerous. Frankie and his gang would do anything to be cool. I'd seen a gun conspicuously lodged in Frankie's waist-band at Gatto's once.

I almost wished Mickey would go back to hanging all over Joey. At least that was respect-able. At least then he had a *chance* of making it before getting himself killed.

What the hell was I thinking? I didn't *want* him to make it! I should be *happy* he was hang-ing out with Frankie. Maybe he'd start to see how stupid he was being, and he'd get back to school. No way could Mickey *like* being around a moron like Frankie. Yech! I felt a little embar-rassed for him. Poor kid, I thought. He's proba-bly confused because a lot of his old friends—the ones he used to hang out with when he was in high school—they're mostly all away at col-lege now. I better have a talk with Mickey to-night.

Erica was clapping her hands in front of my face. "Hey!" she said. "Did you want my notes from English, or what?"

I nodded and started copying. Sucking on another pretzel, I said, "I got a short skirt you could borrow on Saturday. It's too big for me anyway, so you could keep it if it fits."

"Cool," Erica said.

A few minutes later, between pretzels, Erica slapped the table and laughed. "Did you know," she said, "that *Joey Valentino* rhymes with *Vinnie Barbarino*? You're practically going out with a Sweathog!"

Figures Erica, an insomniac like me, would know all the late reruns on cable.

"You're a fucking geek," I said, throwing another pretzel at her.

Chapter Twelve

After school on Thursday, Erica and I started up the steps to her apartment to work on our homework together. I was still avoiding Mickey, especially since seeing him with Frankie. I knew confronting him wouldn't do any good, so I was waiting for him to come to me.

"Oh shit," I said. "I forgot again. Come on over to my house for a second, and you can get that skirt I'm lending you."

"You sure I have to wear a skirt?" Erica complained as she followed me back downstairs. "Couldn't I wear really tight jeans?"

Mickey was in the family room, watching a tape of the movie *Miller's Crossing.* Erica started to lean in to make goo-goo eyes at him, but I grabbed her arm and pulled her to the stairs. In my room we dumped book bags on my bed, and I got out a cigarette.

"God," she said, "my parents would kill me if I smoked in the house!" Meanwhile, she got out her own cigarette.

I shrugged. "So would mine, I guess, but

with Mickey around, it's not likely they'll notice a little smoke."

"I wish I had a brother to take the blame all the time!" Erica said.

"Mickey doesn't get *blamed* for anything, he just gets away with stuff," I said. "And you're not even supposed to be here, since my parents aren't home, so hurry up."

We stood in front of my closet, smoke curling into the crowded rack of clothes. The closet floor was cluttered with shoeboxes filled with half-finished stories I'd written and old collections of stuff like dolls, bottle caps and newspaper clippings about the neighborhood. The rest of my room was neat, but the closet was a minefield of unfinished, uncertain dreams. No story was ever finished, and no collection grew past being a box of somewhat related junk. Like me. Like everyone on my block.

"Here's the skirt," I said, trying not to be depressed.

Passing me her cigarette, Erica yanked off her boots and jeans. "I won't be able to take a deep breath all night, and I could be arrested for bending over in this thing, but I guess it's okay," she said.

The skirt looked great on her and wasn't nearly as tight as she pretended. Erica always talked about being fat, just because her mother looked like a Thanksgiving parade float. She was right about it being a little short—Erica was pretty tall. On me the skirt came to midknee, but on her you could practically see crotch hairs.

"Hey, you never wear this," Erica said, reaching bravely between tightly packed hangers and grabbing a triangle of green rayon. She pulled, and a short-sleeved blouse, the color and wrinkled texture of money, slowly slid out.

"It matches your eyes," she said, holding the blouse against me as she took back her cigarette.

I shrugged. "I never wear it. You can have it."

"Cool," she said. "I'm gonna try it on. Here, hold this."

She handed me her cigarette again. As I took a drag from mine, I suddenly froze. Shushing Erica, I tiptoed quickly to the window and dumped the cigarettes outside. I fanned the air with a pillow, while Erica, in her bra and my skirt, fanned with the green blouse. My father was home from work.

"Are you in big trouble?" Erica asked.

"I *can't* be," I said. "They better not ground me. I'm going out with Joey on Saturday, no matter what! I mean, what's the big deal? I'm seventeen years old, and I should be able to have friends over whenever I want, right?"

Erica patted my shoulder. "It'll be okay. I bet I can sneak out without anyone seeing."

"Yeah," I said. "Pop's probably in his room right now, having a drink and a smoke. Let's go."

Erica pulled her own shirt back on. Her long hair stuck to the back of her neck, but she didn't even take a second to pull it free of the shirt. Grabbing her book bag while I snatched her jeans from the floor, she silently swung the door open and looked both ways. She nodded to me that the hallway was clear, and we tiptoed to the steps.

My foot stopped just before touching the first step when I heard a glass break. Erica and I started backing up to my room when the shouting started.

"Fuck you!" Mickey yelled.

"In *my* house, you'll act like a gentleman," Pop said. "Or I'll wash your mouth out with soap, I swear I will!"

"You mean Ma will. What're you going to do, old man? Fall on me? Poke me with your bony elbow? Fucking kill me with your fucking B.O.? Take a fucking shower!"

A drawer screeched, and I stopped before following Erica into my room. Who was getting what? It didn't sound like the kitchen drawer where Ma kept the wooden spoon.

"Hey, Pop, chill out," Mickey said, his voice quieter now.

"Get out of my sight," Pop said.

"Look, Pop, I was just kidding, you know? Is that thing loaded?"

Then Mickey started chanting a line from *Miller's Crossing*, "I'm praying to you, look in your heart, look in your heart!"

I couldn't tell if he was teasing Pop or if he was really freaking out.

"Get out of my sight," Pop said again.

More glass tinkled and crashed against the hardwood floor as someone bumped a table. I hoped it wasn't one of Ma's glass animals that broke.

Since when did Pop have a gun? Did Ma know?

I backed quickly into my room and shut the door as Mickey came bounding up the stairs. He saw me for an instant and growled. Next second, his door slammed shut so hard, the lamp on my dresser shook and the box in the closet holding my cigarette box collection fell, spilling fifteen different brands onto the rug.

Then it was quiet.

"Guess I'll stay here a while," Erica whispered. "Want to study for that vocabulary test?"

I knew Erica was feeling embarrassed about hearing my family fight. Her normally olive complexion looked suddenly maroon. Because I was a little embarrassed too, I took out my notebook without saying anything.

"You want me to quiz you first?" she asked.

I nodded. Still whispering, she asked me to define *animosity* and use it in a sentence. Before I could answer, the deafening silence that seemed to be surrounding my room was broken by hurried, angry noises that came crashing through the wall separating Mickey from us. I winced and wondered what he was doing.

Should I see what's up with him? I thought.

Erica put down her notebook and changed back into her jeans, not looking at me. Meanwhile, I started to cry. A fat drop fell onto the vocabulary list on my lap, and the paper where it landed softened into a tiny pool of blue ink.

I could hear Mickey's bed scraping the floor, and ripping sounds from our connecting wall. That would be his ancient Heather Locklear poster, I thought. Gently resting a hand on my shoulder, Erica sank to the floor next to me. Her other hand fiddled nervously with the Harley emblem around her neck because we were not the huggy-feely type of friends. But a moment later, as Mickey's door screamed open and slammed shut, she did hug me, and I let her. I couldn't remember the last time I'd been hugged, and it felt so good, my quiet crying turned into bawling.

When I finished crying a minute later, I realized Mickey had probably run away—if you could call it that. I guess an eighteen-year-old just leaves home. I was glad, and already I felt guilty about that.

"Now's a good time for you to sneak out," I said to Erica.

She nodded. "Want to come to my house?"

Although I did want to, I shook my head and helped her stuff everything into her book bag.

Insomnia never comes when you want it. That night, after dinner, I smoked half a pack of cigarettes trying to stay awake, even though it was only eight o'clock. I didn't feel like I'd die in my sleep. I knew I wouldn't, which was almost depressing. If I stayed alive, I'd have to make something of my life.

I fell asleep trying to hear my mother cry. Not that I wanted her to feel unhappy. But I wanted someone to feel unhappy, because I couldn't. I was jealous of Mickey because he'd finally done something he wanted to do, even if it wasn't what *I* wanted him to do. Even if it was stupid and might get him killed. One thing was sure—he wasn't going to die in his sleep.

Chapter Thirteen

On Saturday I left my house as if I was going to work. Instead, I went to the library, all the way down Houston Street. I read magazines until eight and then walked back to Gatto's. Joey was meeting me there.

Erica was busy, so I didn't get to talk to her while I changed in the pantry and touched up my makeup. I decided not to wear my wig. When I was ready, I went outside to wait. I knew Paulie would've let me sit at the bar, but it just would've made customers uncomfortable. Women were not supposed to socialize there.

Most of the trees were already bare, even though it was early in October. The wind whipped sooty leaves against my shins, and I wished I'd worn nylons. But I couldn't do that, because first time I pulled them down to pee I would get a big, ugly run. I'd never been very graceful.

While I waited for Joey, I remembered the last time I'd gone on a date. It was almost six months earlier, before I started working at

Gatto's. Now I was so busy, between work and school and Mickey, it wasn't worth the effort to make time for the boys at school. Especially since they acted so *immature*. I'd always been into older guys, and now that I was a senior, all the older guys were away at college, or worse, playing cards on their mommies' stoops.

Scott Hanson was the first guy I had sex with. He wanted to give me his class ring, but I thought that was dumb because I knew I didn't love him. When he broke up with me I was glad, because I was afraid of taking him home to meet my parents—Scott was half Chinese, and I knew Pop would've had a hissy fit. Anyway, sex with Scott was like making love to a hanger. He was wicked skinny, and his hip bones actually bruised me when he poked in and out.

The only guy, before Joey, who really excited me was one of Mickey's friends since kindergarten. He was in the drama club, and his voice reminded me of Ma's strawberry shortcake. Even though he never noticed me, I still had pictures of Jack that I looked at sometimes when the night was slicing me into pieces. My *what ifs* were soothing and kept me whole. I even had a ball of string Jack once touched that

I kept in my purse. Maybe after tonight, I'd throw it away.

By the time Joey arrived, I was shivering inside, and my head was so soggy with memories, I was speechless. So I just smiled and sank into the warm, leathery front seat. I hoped I looked good enough to be next to Joey. He smelled musky with experience and looked like a god, only in a double-breasted, straight out of *Newsday*'s John Gotti fashion drawings, silk-blend suit instead of a toga. Though a toga would've looked great too—I'd like to see Joey's bare legs. I just knew they were tan, with a soft coat of lightly curling hair.

"What are you thinking?" he said, smiling and showing off shiny teeth I could almost see my reflection in.

"Nothing!" I said, and turned to the window so he wouldn't see me blush.

Joey took me to a place in Bensonhurst, Brooklyn. I'd never been that far away from my own neighborhood, so it would have been thrilling even without Joey next to me. As it was, I felt like royalty. It was like Joey knew everyone. We got a table by the window without having to wait, even though there was a line at the door.

Joey ordered a scotch, and I ordered a Bloody

Mary. Instantly I regretted it, thinking it wasn't really a dinner drink and ordering it showed my age. Thank God the waiter didn't proof me. I wondered if Joey knew I was still in high school, and if he cared.

The menu was written all in Italian, of which I knew very little. So I chose what I thought was linguini with meat sauce and hoped for the best. After ordering, I wondered if I should have picked something less likely to drip and stain my white blouse. When we ate spaghetti at home, we wore spaghetti shirts, which were old shirts of Pop's we kept in the kitchen pantry for pasta dinners.

Joey and I had exhausted all possible combinations of small talk on the long drive out of Manhattan. We'd discussed the weather, not only in New York, but in the Midwest and Northwest as well. We'd talked about the Yankees and inflation. So now, partly because I'd finished my Bloody Mary and was feeling less nervous, I told Joey about my family's spaghetti shirts. He laughed, and I felt like I could start breathing again. When the waiter came with our salads, I ordered a martini, which I'd never had before, but which I thought was a sophisticated thing to drink. Anyway, I liked olives. I asked for two.

Joey delicately cut his salad of big, leafy greens into small pieces, and I imitated him. As he speared a piece of endive with his fork, he smiled at me. I felt clumsy, dumb and stupid, sitting across from his urbane perfection.

But he saved me by talking with his mouth full. "Bet you meet a lot of interesting people at Mario's place," he said.

I loved that a small piece of salad slid out of his mouth and hung on the corner of his lip. It was very human and, I thought, very sexy. I was feeling pretty confident and took a big sip of my martini.

If only a martini tasted as good as it looked! I could barely keep from wincing as I forced myself to swallow. It tasted like cough medicine without the sweet cherry flavor. If I had ordered a glass of liquid propane, I would've expected it to taste better than this! Quickly plowing a forkful of radicchio into my mouth, I almost forgot that Joey had spoken to me and I should answer.

Gulping the last of the water in my goblet, I said, "Yeah, I meet a lot of people, I guess. Not that I really get to talk to anyone for a long time. Just 'hello, good-bye,' mostly."

Joey licked his lips, clearing away the piece of

endive that had been stuck there. Someone called out, "Joey! How are ya? Haven't seen you in a while!"

Joey turned to shake hands with the speaker, and I dumped half my martini into my empty water goblet. Then I sipped what was left in the martini glass, hoping I would have already acquired a taste for it. Unfortunately, the second sip was even worse than the first. I covered the bottom of my face with my napkin, because this time I couldn't help grimacing.

"Sorry," Joey said. "Tony lives upstairs from me, but I've been spending so much time in Manhattan lately, seems like I never see anyone from around here anymore."

"Don't they have work to do in the city too?" I asked.

Joey looked at me funny for a second, or maybe it was just my imagination. Then he laughed. "Naah," he said, "I don't think Tony ever worked in his life."

I smiled, and chewed, and thought to myself that Tony looked more like a cop than a gangster.

"Except if you call stealing hubcaps working!" Joey said, laughing again.

I relaxed, glad Tony was just a thief and not a

cop. Cops always made me feel like I'd done something wrong.

The busboy came and refilled my water goblet, and I sipped it cautiously. I found that the martini didn't taste so bad, watered down like that, and took a big gulp. My gut, which had been a little queasy, started to feel warm, and I was looking forward to the main course. Now that my hands weren't shaking so much, I felt like I might manage to eat without coming out looking like an expressionist painting *Tomato Sauce on Silk, #1.*

"Boy, that Mario's a character, huh?" Joey said as our salad plates were cleared.

"Yeah," I said. "He looks like a cat, doesn't he?"

Joey laughed. I wondered if he was as nervous as me. I wondered, if he took his suit jacket off, would there be sweat stains in the armpits? I could feel cool droplets sliding over my own skin.

"I bet you hear all kinds of stuff, working at Mario's," Joey said. "I bet you know more about him than anyone, just from what you hear delivering drinks."

I shrugged. I didn't know Joey well enough to tell him I wanted to write a book.

I was glad when our food came and Joey stopped talking about Gatto's. I was beginning to feel like I was being interviewed, or even interrogated. I thought Joey was a big shot. I thought he knew *everything*.

Probably he was just nervous, like me, and he couldn't think of anything else to talk about. We had Gatto's in common. During the main course, Joey started talking about his grandfather's farm in Illinois, and I relaxed. We shared a cannoli for dessert, and I had a glass of port, which felt just as sophisticated as a martini and tasted better.

We left the restaurant at eleven-thirty. As we waited for Joey's car to be brought around, I saw someone with a curly mop of hair just like Mickey's getting out of a car across the street. Before I could squint against the dark and see better, Joey's car was in front of me and Joey was holding my door open. It couldn't have been him anyway, I thought. Mickey wasn't likely to ever go more than six blocks from home, even if it wasn't, technically, his home anymore. Even so, it was strange I hadn't seen him around since he'd left . . .

I decided not to worry so much and leaned

back into the soft leather of Joey's Mercedes. We decided to swing past Gatto's, which Joey now also called Mario's place. I hoped he wouldn't tell Mario!

Joey said he had someone he had to see. I hoped I'd get to see Erica.

Chapter Fourteen

When we got to Gatto's, Joey asked me to wait in the car. I was annoyed, but I didn't say anything. Squinting, I studied the club's shaded window, trying to see if it was busy in there tonight, and how Erica was doing. Everything was dark, muffled shapes. Leaning back in my seat, I bit my lower lip and folded my arms over my chest. I knew it wouldn't have been cool for Joey to bring me in with him, but all I wanted was one little peek!

I was still pouting when Joey came out of the club. Swaggering close behind him was a skinny guy I'd seen him with before. I always thought he was just another wannabe, tagging along, but he and Joey seemed pretty chummy now. Fucking great, I thought. Joey will probably be taking me home now, so he can deal with business.

Then the skinny guy paused and opened the door again. He leaned in and yelled something, and an instant later, the door swung open as Erica bounced out. Even from where I was sitting in the car, I could see a happy glaze over her eyes. She tossed an arm around Skinny's waist and waved at me with her free hand.

I opened my window, and Erica stuck her head in as far as it would go. She smelled like tequila. Obviously I shouldn't have worried about her.

"Catherine, I want you to meet my new friend, Sally," she said. "Isn't that the cutest name for a guy?"

I nodded. "Are you off work now?" I asked.

"Yeah," she said. "Sally's a friend of Joey's! Isn't that the coolest! Now we can double-date!"

Joey was laughing as he got into the car. "You could talk from the backseat, you know," he said. "Get the fuck in the car already, you deadbeats!"

"I got a tape we could listen to," Erica said after we got going. "Put this in."

Joey took the tape from her and snapped it into the tape deck without looking to see what it was. It was funny the way he cringed when Melissa Etheridge's latest album screamed from the speakers. I didn't know of many guys who liked Melissa. Erica and I thought she was the best. Her and Pat Benatar. Wonder what Joey would've done if Erica had slipped him Pat Benatar's best-of tape.

Between what Erica had probably consumed in tequila and all the vodka I'd slurped down between courses during dinner, we didn't care much if Sally and Joey liked our music. We sang "American Girl" as loudly as we could. Luckily Joey had a great stereo, and the music drowned out our voices. By the time the song ended, we were parking the car in Chelsea, around the corner from the Snakepit dance club.

Erica and I walked ahead, talking about our nights. When I told her about the martini, she asked if I ate the olives.

"They were totally gross," I said. "How'd you meet Sally?"

"He pinched my butt," she said. "And he asked if I liked to get high."

I was about to ask her more, but we were already at the club. Ugh! I thought. There was a line a block long outside.

"Maybe we should try someplace else," I said to Joey when he and Sally caught up.

Sally nudged Joey in the ribs and cackled like a girl. "I don't see no line," he said.

Joey just smiled and held my hand. He pulled me through the clump of people near the door and waved to the doorman. Inside the door, a woman with poufy frosted hair looked up from her clipboard. Joey gave her a kiss on the cheek, and we were in. Tonight was Eighties

97

Night, and I heard Blondie singing at the end of the long, dark hallway that led into the belly of the club. The walls were carpeted.

The main floor of Snakepit was crowded with swaying bodies. The flashing colored lights and smoky haze blinded me at first, and I let myself be led by the arm to the bar. Despite the crowd, four empty stools appeared for us. While Joey ordered drinks—Please don't order me a martini, I thought—I concentrated on the crowd. Then I looked at Erica, cringing. I was a little hurt when she didn't grimace back at me. Instead, she shrugged and giggled.

"It's Wannabe Central!" I said. God, I thought, why did Joey bring us here? Wasn't he disgusted? I never saw so many tacky gold chains and hairy, exposed chests in my life.

"Do you think the bodyguards have to pay their own way in?" Erica said.

A cigarette girl stopped by, and I reached in my purse for money, while Erica grabbed two boxes of Marlboro Lights. The girl waved our money away and smiled at Joey and Sally. Evidently they were the king and duke of the wannabes. I began to feel more comfortable. It wasn't like *I* was one of those pathetic girls with the long, bleached, permed hair, stiff with hairspray. *I* wasn't sleeping with every guy who had a Porsche or Mustang convertible, a gold pinky ring and a thick, stupid accent. *I* wasn't holding one guy's hand while winking at his bodyguard. I was even planning on finishing high school, with honors, which certainly set me apart from this crew.

Girls were looking at Erica and me like they wanted to kill us as we threw back shots of tequila with Joey and Sally. Although I felt funny to be wearing a black leather vest over my silk blouse, I was proud. I knew that because I wasn't wearing something with shiny tassels and sequins, I wouldn't have gotten into Snakepit without Joey, but I was proud to be sitting next to him. I wished he would nibble on my ear or something, but he and Sally were talking.

Erica gestured to me with her head to follow her. Together we shoved through schmoozing cliques of people who weren't even organized enough to be gangs. We waited on line at the bathroom, trying to ignore the funny looks. I almost wished I was wearing my long wig, so I could pouf it up with hairspray. Wasted as she was, Erica shook her hair around as though she belonged here. We both knew that neither of us did. This better be important, I thought, as I began to get pissed at Erica for taking me away from the bar, where everyone idolized us.

We got to the front of the line, and Erica pulled me into the bathroom with her. The girl behind me gave us a nasty look, so Erica gave her the finger.

"Look what Sally gave me," she said.

She had a folded piece of paper from a magazine page in her hand. Pulling out a flap, she poured white powder onto the toilet seat. Now I knew why she was so easygoing tonight. She was tweaked. I rolled a twenty quickly and snorted about half—probably a little more. My eyes watered for a second, and then my head cleared. I'd been starting to feel pretty drunk, but now I could focus again. The bitter numbness in the back of my throat made me feel like gagging a little, and someone was pounding on the door, so we hurried out, back to the bar. I felt that same intense sense of belonging I felt the first time I did coke, and it felt *right*.

"Don't tell Joey," Erica said. "Sally says Joey doesn't know he deals."

"Are you kidding?" I said. "Make sure *Sally* doesn't tell Joey *I'm* doing lines!"

"So now we finally have a drug connection!" Erica whispered as we slid onto our barstools.

I shrugged. I mean, the coke was great, but I didn't think I needed a "connection." Especially because there was no way I was ever going to *pay* for it! It was the perfect thing to have tonight, though. Already the wannabes and their girlfriends didn't seem so retarded.

Joey was talking to an older guy—about forty, I guess. The guy had a gold Italian horn dangling from his neck, and two gold link bracelets on his wrist. His hair was gray at the sideburns and slicked back. A half-starved-looking girl who was probably about my age hung like a rag over his shoulder. She was leaning forward so you could see the tops of her nipples in the hollow between her loose blouse and her ribs. She was fluttering her eyelashes at Sally, who had his hand on her butt.

Erica saw too, and shrugged. "It's not like I'm gonna marry the guy," she said. "I just want to get into cool places and snort free drugs while drinking free drinks. If I'm any good at this, maybe Sally will buy me a Harley someday!"

Whoa, I thought. Is that my next-door neighbor talking? But Erica had always been tougher than me. At least she knew what she wanted. I had to admire her focus.

"You know I'm saving myself for Mickey," she said, winking.

I rolled my eyes at her. "Like I'd let you anywhere near him."

"Like you could find him!" she said.

She might as well have poked me in the eye. I slurped my piña colada and slammed it onto the bar to get the bartender's attention. Erica placed a hand on my shoulder.

"I'm sorry. I was only kidding," she said.

Sticking an ice cube in my mouth, I sucked on it. Yeah, I guess I should forgive her, I thought. After all, her date's feeling up an anorexic bimbo over there. Between that, the tequila, a night at Gatto's, and who-knew-how-much cocaine, I couldn't fairly blame Erica for anything.

I heard a familiar guitar riff shriek through the sound system. "Pat Benatar!" I said.

The song was "All Fired Up," and it felt perfect. We started swinging our hips and singing along, "I believe there comes a time/When everything just falls in line . . ." Suddenly Erica pulled me out onto the dance floor. I'd never felt happier, especially when Joey and Sally squirmed in next to us before the song ended. People made space for Erica and me to flail our arms, and Joey and I banged hip bones to the beat. Everything seemed just right. I wished I could stay there all night. I was almost jealous of all the losers filling the space around our clique. It must be nice to party and pose all the time, without worrying about school or where your life was heading—your biggest worry being what gang to belong to and what crime family to aspire to. Maybe Mickey had it right all along. Maybe he knew the key to happiness—to dance all night and not give a fuck.

Chapter Fifteen

I'm like really fucking beat when I finish at Mario's on Saturday. Joey needed Paulie again for something, so I got stuck dusting all the bottles behind the bar, and cleaning the grill in back, which pissed me off big-time, because it seems to me that dude Joe should have been doing that instead of leaning back in a chair, picking his toes and getting in my way. But I gotta show I'm a good guy, so I couldn't complain.

As I'm cleaning black, oily shit from under my fingernails, I'm thinking, Pretty soon Joey'll take *me* out on a job, instead of Paulie. I mean, he *better*. I'm not going for this honest day's work shit forever, you know? At least I got paid sixty dollars for today. Could be worse.

When I leave Mario's, it's like fucking forty degrees out, and I'm thinking, Motherfucker, I don't want to be sleeping by the Dumpster tonight. It's too fucking cold. But no way am I going back home and apologizing to Pop. Like he has any right to fuck with me, when he can't even drive a garbage truck straight, he's so fucking drunk all the time. Fucking pointing a gun at me—who the fuck does he think he is?

So I go back behind Mario's, where the big, black Dumpster is, and I start fishing through my duffel bag for some warmer socks and shit. There's a noise behind me that sounds like a gunshot, so I drop to the ground, scraping my fucking knuckles against the rusty edge of the Dumpster. When I notice blood on my hand, for a second I think maybe I'm shot, but then I can tell it's just my knuckles are bleeding. I look up at the person who's helping me to my feet, and I see it's only Joey.

"I didn't mean to scare you," he says, "but Mario told me to take care of some bum who's been sleeping out back—his words, not mine. I didn't know it was you."

I shove my hands in my pockets and throw my shoulders back. Blowing a curl off my forehead, I say, "It ain't like I'm *sleeping* out here, I just keep my stuff here during the day. I'm sort of in between residences at the moment, you know?"

"Where are you staying tonight? I could give you a ride."

"Naah," I say, looking down. "I was thinking of maybe grabbing a beer or something first. But thanks."

Joey looks me over for a second and then says, "You know, I've got a spare room and a fold-out couch at my place in Brooklyn. Why don't you come out there with me tonight? You don't have to stay if you have stuff to do, but you could at least keep your stuff there. Mario's gonna have a hissy fit if he finds that shit out here again."

I can feel my heart beating like crazy, I'm so fucking excited. Stay at Joey Valentino's? Fuckin' A, where do I sign up? And anyway, it's not like I could stay here and piss off Mario. Like they say in *The Godfather*, Joey's making me an offer I can't refuse.

When I thank Joey and get into his car, I'm expecting him to say, "Someday, and that day may never come, I will ask you to do a service," like Marlon Brando said to the undertaker.

But he's pretty quiet until we get to his place. He doesn't even get pissed at the traffic on the BQE, even though I'm giving drivers the finger on all sides. When someone gestures back at me, I think, Asshole, you don't know who you're fucking with. One word to my friend Joey here and he'll blow your fucking head off! Man, this is the life. Wait till I tell the guys.

Wait till I tell *Frankie*—goddamn, he'll be jealous! This is so sweet!

Joey even lets me take the first shower. I hope it's not just because he doesn't want me to stink up his house. But I can understand his point of view. I mean, I went into the living room, and there was all this fucking awesome furniture, with like velvet upholstery and dark wood. And it was all just out there, exposed, with no plastic covers or anything like we have at home. That's class, I think.

After showering, I help myself to some scotch, and I drink it straight. This is it, I think, I'm making the big time. The scotch kind of burns, but you can't drink beer in a place like Joey's, it wouldn't fit in. Even Southern Comfort, which is what me and the guys drink when we're hangin', is too sweet for this place. I never thought so, but maybe Catherine's right, Southern Comfort is a girlie drink.

"I'm going out. If you need them, there's a spare set of keys hanging by the door," Joey says, coming downstairs as he fastens his tie.

"Hot date?" I ask, feeling kind of chummy.

Joey just looks at me, and I look at the floor.

I'm sorry, I feel like saying, but I thought we were buddies!

"It's nothing personal—" Joey starts to say.

"—it's just business," I finish for him in my head.

"—but I'm late already," Joey says. "There's linguini my mother made in the fridge. Also, maybe you should try calling home. Someone might be worried."

As Joey leaves, I'm saying to myself in a pretty good Brando imitation, "A man who doesn't spend time with his family can never be a real man."

The important thing is to find the right family, I think.

Chapter Sixteen

Erica and I tiptoed into my bedroom at three in the morning. The cocaine I did at Snakepit had made my dinner settle into a heavy, rumbling lump in my stomach. Several times at the club, whenever I wasn't dancing or sucking down a drink, I felt like vomiting, but I kept the food down by sipping another cool beer. Now that I was home, nausea slid over me again, and I hurried to the bathroom. If I hadn't been so wasted, I would've been embarrassed for Erica to hear me puke. Tonight I didn't care. I just wanted to get rid of the lump in my belly.

Afterward I brushed my teeth and wiped drops of slop from my leather vest. Erica had taken my mirror from the wall and was laying out two skinny lines.

"Do you think we should?" I asked, although I'd been thinking as I brushed my teeth that another line would feel good, especially now that my stomach was comfortably empty.

"Just one more," Erica said. "To take the slur off those last shots we did. I'm feeling woozy."

When I snorted the line, my nostril didn't even burn. It had been desensitized by the five lines I'd done earlier. I had a feeling I was going to be miserable when morning came, but that was inevitable at this point. One more line wouldn't change how I'd feel later.

My hand shook as I lit a cigarette. "I hope I didn't embarrass myself tonight," I said. "Sometimes I felt like I couldn't stop talking. Do you think Joey knew?"

"Naah," Erica said. "You didn't sound that wasted to me. Hey, where's that bottle of brandy I picked up for you? Got any glasses?"

I got two Dixie cups from the bathroom and pulled the brandy out from under a pile of assorted old sneakers—circa 1988 to 1996—in my closet.

"I can't believe we're gonna do it!" Erica said. "It'll be so much fun, the two of us working together, even if the club's full of losers."

We had been offered jobs as cigarette girls at Snakepit by the owner. He was the guy with the gray sideburns and waif girlfriend Joey had spent so much time talking to.

It was after one when Joey led me through the smelly weeds of people, and I'd had just enough coke and tequila to feel like a white rose, just picked, after it's bloomed and long before it's begun to wither. My face was flushed, but otherwise I felt pure and smooth. As Joey held my hand in his large, firm fingers and directed me through a green door into a dark hallway, I licked my lips, anticipating his tongue.

"Mario's club is dangerous," he said.

That took me by surprise. My thorns prickled to attention and I almost told him I didn't need a keeper. But when he touched my hair and blinked his sexy blue eyes, I felt flattered that he cared.

Maybe he caught my initial stiffening, because he said, "Of course, you handle yourself well, so I'm not worried . . ."

"The tips are good," I said softly, mesmerized by those deep blue sparkling eyes and soft pink lips.

". . . but I was thinking, it must be boring, all those old guys who don't talk. You'd be happier at a place like this, right?"

I could only shrug. I mean, I guess the music was pretty good. But I really wanted to be wherever Joey was.

Joey smiled. "All right, I'll be straight. See, I do a lot of . . . business . . . at Mario's, and if you're there, I might feel . . . distracted."

"You want me to work here?" I asked.

Joey squeezed my shoulder and opened another green door. The owner guy, Ron, sat behind a big desk. He looked up with wide, almost frightened eyes, then chilled out when he saw Joey.

"You wanna work here, babe?" he asked me.

Joey's fingers tightened a little on my shoulder, which I didn't understand, because I thought Ron was his buddy.

"Next Friday. Eight o'clock," Ron said.

"What about my friend Erica, could you—"

"Next Friday. Eight o'clock."

"If everything Joey said is true, and I don't see why he'd lie to me, then I won't be at Gatto's much longer. It's too bad. I was starting to like it there," I said to Erica.

Besides telling me *his* reasons for me working at Snakepit, Joey had told me that Mario's niece—Frankie's sister—had just turned sixteen and wanted a job. Minnie Mouse, as we called her behind her back at school, actually looked more like a rat than a mouse. When she stood next to Mario the Cat, you expected him to pounce and eat her alive. I couldn't see her surviving at his club, with her pointy face, long nose and beady eyes, but family is family.

"This is so fucking wild," Erica said. "And I need the money, too. I have a feeling Sally won't ever come through with a Harley, and it's looking like my father—the bastard—still has a lot of years left in his miserable life, and anyway, when he dies, after all his bimbos get through, there won't be any money left for me anyway. Why didn't someone blow him away before I was old enough to remember him? Anyway, I guess I'll have to save my own money for a bike."

"Your dad still hits you?" I asked.

Erica shrugged. "Not so much, I guess. For one thing, I stay clear when he's in a mood. For another thing, I've been working out so much, I think he's getting scared of me. I'm only an inch shorter than him now, and I bet my shoulders are wider. If he ever punches me again, I'll knock his head off. That's what I told him last time."

Erica poured herself another cup of brandy. The thin paper looked soggy and was barely still in a cup shape.

I felt warm and comfortable, even though the coke had me shivering and my eyes were bugging out. Erica never said as much about her life as just now. We always just figured things out about each other, but we hardly ever talked. Cocaine was great that way—it made it easier to be honest, even sentimental. I gave Erica a hug, and blackberry brandy spilled onto her knee.

"Whoops," I said.

She shrugged and went into the bathroom for a new cup.

"How much of that stuff is left?" I asked.

"Lots," she said, wiping her leg with toilet paper. "Sally gave me practically a gram. Want some more?"

She cut two more lines, a little thicker than before. Deep down, I knew I didn't need any more, but the taste was already gone from the back of my throat, and I missed it.

"Could I get some for a rainy day?" I asked.

Erica showed me how to fold a quarter of a page of notebook paper into a neat packet, and dumped two big rocks in. Sliding my arm under my dresser, I retrieved my money envelope and put the coke stash in there.

"Have you heard from your brother?" Erica asked. She looked down into her cup.

"Uh-uh," I said, lighting another cigarette. "I haven't even seen him around since we saw him with Frankie on Monday. Weird, huh?"

"Think he's okay?"

Shrugging, I said, "I hope so. I mean, I'm sure he is. We'd hear if he wasn't, right? I kind of wish he'd call, but I kind of don't want to talk to him either. I just wish he'd go back to college, or get a life or something!"

Erica played with her cup, unrolling the paper lip between her fingers. Finally she said, "I heard Sally mention him tonight at Gatto's, before we ended up being friendly."

"He's not in trouble, is he?" I asked, trying not to sound worried or motherly. "I'll kill him if he's fucking up!" I almost thought I was going to cry for a second, but I was too high on coke.

"What if he's already too fucked up?" Erica asked, barely meeting my eyes.

"It's only been like a week, how screwy could he be?"

Erica shrugged. "I don't know. I hope it's not true, but I got the feeling from what I heard that Mickey might be dealing or something like that."

"What's 'something like that' mean?" I said, a little too loudly. Erica cringed, and I felt bad. It wasn't her fault if my brother was an idiot and I had a rescue complex.

"I don't know," Erica said. "I heard Sally and some other guys talking about Frankie and his crew. They thought it was 'cute'—that's what they said—that Frankie picked up six grams, just so long as he wasn't moving in on the real business and he kept his mouth shut. One of the guys said Frankie knew about keeping his mouth shut, and someone said Mickey's name, like they were wondering about his reputation, or if he might mean trouble or something. Cat, I really don't know that much. It's just something I heard, real quick. Maybe I didn't even hear Mickey's name."

"It's okay," I said. "Thanks for telling me. I guess it doesn't matter. There's nothing I can do about it. Mickey's a big boy. He'll take care of himself. Excuse me a second."

I went into the bathroom and shut the door behind me. The blackberry brandy tasted sour as I threw it up into the toilet. I suddenly wished I hadn't done any more coke after leaving the club, so maybe I'd be falling asleep now, even if it meant having bed-spins from all the drinking I did. Leaning my cheek against the toilet rim, I wondered if Mickey was sleeping right now. What about Joey? Was he home in Bensonhurst already? Did I have the guts to shoot Frankie in the head? How was I going to survive the next ten months until I could get out of this place?

As I flushed the toilet, I thought, It's not really any of my business, not even what's going to happen to *me,* and especially not what's going to happen to Mickey. Things will just happen, that's all. I went into Mickey's room and got his deck of cards and poker chips out of his desk drawer.

"Five-card stud?" I asked Erica, who was doing another line.

"How 'bout we play for real money?" she said. "Make it interesting!"

Chapter Seventeen

The third Saturday in October, I was supposed to take the SATs for the second time. Even though I got 1100 my first time, last spring, Ma said she knew I could do better if I studied this time, especially on the math section. Because my grades were all good, I didn't think I needed a better SAT score, but whatever Ma wanted, I always did, eventually.

It was the Tuesday before the exam, and after school I was supposed to take the last of my SAT review classes. All I wanted to do was go home and sleep. My body wasn't used to partying like I had on Saturday night, and my stomach had been upset ever since Sunday's hangover. Making matters worse, that day was a gym day, and we had to start class with twenty laps around the gym. As I tied my old, holey sneakers, I wondered if I'd make it.

I started at a slow jog—as close as I could get to just walking—and Erica had passed me three times before I finished my first lap. Ms. Jones, the gym teacher, frowned at me and tapped her stopwatch as I shuffled past. She lifted her knees up high, jogging a few paces in place, indicating that I should do the same. Screw her, I thought, I get shin splints from running. It would help if I had a good pair of sneakers, but I wasn't going to spend my hard-earned cash on *sneakers,* for God's sake! Neither was Ma.

After her ninth lap and halfway through my fifth, Erica slowed down next to me. She had to lift her knees high just to keep from passing me again, her legs were so long. I wondered how she could be in such great shape when she smoked at least as many cigarettes as I did. I asked her.

"I gotta be in shape at my house," she said. "Otherwise, how would I keep my father from popping me one? I got to let him see that I have muscles too! You better watch it, or you'll end up looking fat and soggy, like my mom."

"I've barely eaten anything since Saturday night," I said, sucking air. A cramp was pinching at my side.

Erica sped up and passed me again. She caught up with me as I passed Ms. Jones at the starting line. She blew a kiss at Ms. Jones when she wasn't looking, and I almost choked from laughing while running. My chuckle came out as painful gasps, and I still had fifteen laps to go.

"You got anything left out of that stuff I gave

you?" Erica asked, still breathing almost normally. "I finished mine last night."

"No," I lied. I felt guilty at once, because she was my best friend. But I didn't want her to think I couldn't handle as much coke as her. I didn't want to share what I had left either, which I had a feeling was why she was asking me. I liked to collect and save things for a rainy day. Erica like to use things up and move on.

"That's too bad," Erica said, "because I was hoping to borrow a line until this afternoon."

"What's happening this afternoon?"

Erica smiled, and I noticed she had perfectly white teeth, unlike mine, which were nicotine yellow. Her teeth didn't used to be that good.

When she noticed I was staring, she said, "I started brushing my teeth with baking soda to get rid of the stains. Sally told me that was his secret. Whatcha doing after school? Me and Sally are going down to Coney Island. He's got some business, and then we're going to cruise along the boardwalk, shit like that, you know, nothing special."

"Can't," I said. "I gotta go to that SAT class. It's the last one."

"You could skip it," Erica said.

Wiping sweat from my eyebrows with the

sleeve of my T-shirt, I said, "Naah, I better not. I promised my ma. Sally getting more of that stuff for you?"

"Yeah, want me to get you some? He might make me pay for it, since he knows now that I don't want to sleep with him. Give me twenty bucks?"

"Tomorrow," I said, finishing my seventh lap. I felt bad that she was thinking of me, when I'd been so stingy before. I wanted to offer her what I had left, which was in my blush compact in the locker room. But then she'd know I'd lied to her before. I vowed to make it up to her some other time.

"I better run," Erica said, jabbing me in the ribs with her elbow. My cramp got worse, and now I felt a little like throwing up.

"I want to finish with a good time. I still want to set a new record for the school before Christmas," Erica said as she started pumping her legs faster. She made up for the time she'd wasted talking to me and passed me four times during my next lap.

"Be careful with that guy," I said as she pounded past me again. I wasn't sure if she'd heard me. I was so out of breath at that point, my voice was high-pitched and breathy, and not very clear.

But next time around, Erica said, "Look who's talking, *Mrs. Valentino!*"

If I could've caught her, I would've kicked her in the butt for that. Although when I thought about it, *Mrs. Valentino* had a nice ring to it. We'd have beautiful children, with my green eyes and perky nose and Joey's long lashes and hot butt.

I was so sleepy by the end of the day, I pinched two half-moons with my fingernails into the soft skin between my thumb and hand to stay awake in advanced calculus. After class, I noticed that the marks were still there and were turning purple.

I refused to do drugs during school, but, I reasoned, this was after school, so I went into the bathroom and got a razor blade and the packet of coke out of my Revlon blush compact. After cleaning the mirrored part with some toilet paper, I sliced a thick piece off the rock in the packet and cut it up on the mirror. A little piece popped off onto the floor. When I found it, I picked it up delicately with a moist fingertip and put it under my tongue. It tasted good.

As I chopped the coke, my hands were shaking. This wasn't like smoking in the bathroom, which Erica and I did all the time. If I got caught doing cocaine in the school bathroom, I could kiss my ass good-bye. Although, I thought, at least then I wouldn't have to go to the SAT review class, or even take the test on Saturday morning. Maybe I'd become Mrs. Valentino.

Not likely—Joey hadn't even tongue-kissed me the weekend before. I chopped faster, then rolled a dollar bill and shoved it up my nose so fast, I almost gave myself a paper cut in the nostril. I really hoped this thing with Joey wasn't going to turn into a rotten memory, like my pathetic longings for Mickey's old friend Jack. I was real sick of losing my mind to potential best lovers and them not wanting me the same way. Please, God, I prayed, don't let Joey become a substitute older brother—one is all I can handle.

By the time I left the bathroom, after smoking a cigarette down to the filter, I wasn't tired anymore. My head felt clear, and I was looking forward to taking the practice exam—math section—today. If only I could have a glass of wine with that.

The test was a breeze. On previous practice tests, and the last time I took the whole exam, I'd gotten tired and confused after about twenty questions. The numbers started to swim together, and I had to really concentrate on whether I was supposed to add or subtract or what. But today each question stood out as a single unit, and the numbers seemed to arrange themselves in my mind with very little effort on my part. I finished early and slipped out to the bathroom to do another line. I could take my time now, because only the janitors were left in the building, except for everyone who was still working on the practice test.

My heart was beating fast against my ribs while I waited for everyone to be done so we could go over the answers. Feeling a little sick to my stomach, I wished we'd get on with it. What a bunch of losers, I thought. Just write down *anything*, let's *go!*

Finally time was up. I didn't do as well as I thought I'd done, but I did get my highest score yet. As I left school, jumping down the steps three at a time, I thought that everything I'd ever been taught about coke was a lie. Lies made up to make life harder, when the cocaine made things so much easier. I guess if you were one of those people who did three hundred dollars of coke a day, it was bad, but a line here and there was looking pretty good to me. I hoped Erica would be able to get me something from Sally, because I didn't think the small stash I had left would last until the SATs on Saturday morning.

Chapter Eighteen

"So, you like my sister, huh?"

Joey sips from his scotch, and I help myself to another one because, after all, he's seeing my sister. I have rights.

"She's a sweet girl," Joey says.

"Yeah," I go, "Cat's pretty cool. Does she talk about me?"

Joey just shrugs.

"You gonna see her tonight?"

Joey shrugs again, and I'm starting to get pissed off. I mean, like, she's my sister! And another thing, I'm thinking, If Cat's good enough to take out, when am I gonna be good enough for some real wiseguy work? Hanging out with Frankie and his crew's cool, but it's getting about time I should be hanging with the big guys. If Joey doesn't get on the ball, I'm gonna be out of here, man, and then he'll be sorry. Everyone'll be sorry when I make it.

Then, out of nowhere, Joey goes, "Cathy seems a little . . . confused sometimes."

I have to chuckle. "Yeah, right, man," I say. "Cat's 'confused,' and I'm John Gotti."

Joey's quiet for a second, and then he has the *nerve* to say, "She could use a big brother."

I'm like, "Well, *you're* her *boyfriend* . . ."

And Joey cuts me off. "We're very close . . . friends," he says, and stares at me like it's not my business.

"So if you're so close, *you* unconfuse her!"

"I'd hate to see Cathy get hurt."

"So don't hurt her!" I say, really getting pissed now.

I grit my teeth and suck at my scotch hard, while Joey stares just long enough to start to scare me. Then, typical cool Joey, he shrugs.

"You going out tonight?" he asks.

I shrug. "Naah, I don't know. I was thinking of watching a movie or something. Unless you got something for me to do, then I . . ."

Standing fast, Joey just looks at me, and I think, I've seen that look. Ma and Cat are always looking at me that way, like I'm a little kid and my nose is running. I feel like saying, There's nothing wrong with dreaming, is there? Just because I don't want to be what everyone thinks I should be—there's nothing wrong with that! Goddamn it, I wish people would just let me be what I want to be, maybe even help out now and then. Is something wrong with that?

127

Suddenly I can't wait for Joey to leave. He's just a shithead *user* like everyone else. I should have gone straight to the top. I should have gone to Mario.

"I won't be late," Joey says.

I just shrug. I mean, like, whatever. I'm a big boy now, thank you very much. Fuck off and die.

"Tell Cat I said hi," I say.

"She misses you," Joey says as he heads for the door.

Suddenly I stand up taller and stick my chest out. "You better treat her right," I say.

Joey smiles. "I treat everyone right, don't I?" he says.

A little while later, I'm waiting for Frankie and some other guys in the crew to come over with the beer and a movie. I told him to bring *Goodfellas*. He fucking better!

When Joey's out and I got nothing to do, like now, I like to check out his stuff. Man, he has the coolest outfits ever. I put on a blue wool jacket and button it over my T-shirt. I look hot. Suddenly I'm singing "Rags to Riches," that song that plays in the beginning of *Goodfellas*, and I'm strutting around Joey's bedroom, checking myself out in the mirror and thinking how it'll be when I can visit Ma and Pop and Catherine dressed like this, with a big wad of hundreds in my pocket. I'm gonna be a somebody in a neighborhood full of nobodies.

The doorbell rings, and I freak out, trying to put everything back where I found it. But it turns out it's only Fat Frankie.

"Geez, Frankie," I say as I open the door for him, Angel, Tony and Paul, "you gotta lay off the Cheez Puffs and start working out, like me."

I make a muscle and tighten my belly so when Frankie punches me it doesn't even hurt. Not much, anyway.

"At least I got laid last night, how about you, hotshot?"

I shrug and say, "I'm too busy for that shit. You know, Joey always has me workin' on something."

"Yeah, right," Frankie says, and I don't punch him like I want to because there's four of them and only one of me.

"Hey! My uncle Bennie steals shrimps and lobsters too!" Frankie brags while watching the movie. Like he's more of a goodfella than me.

129

". . . funny like I'm a clown, like I amuse you, like I'm here to fucking amuse you?" we all say together with Joe Pesci, and then we laugh and clink our glasses of scotch together.

"Hey, Tony, I didn't know your mother was a movie star!" Frankie says, pointing at one of the mob wives with the bad eye makeup and cheap clothes on the screen.

"Now *that* gets me in the mood," Frankie says when Henry Hill's girlfriend is pouring a bag of cocaine into the blender to cut it.

Frankie stops the VCR, and I yell, "Hey!"

He smiles and says, "You got a blender, Mickey?"

"How the fuck should I know?"

"You live here, don't you?"

"Yeah, but I ain't the fucking *cook*!"

Next thing I know, Frankie's dumping a Baggie of coke into Joey's blender, and then rubs his finger in the Baggie. Shoving his fat middle finger in my face, he goes, "Lick it," so I do.

My mouth is numb right away, which is really cool.

"You've done blow before, right Mick?" Tony says.

"Of course he has, asshole!" Frankie says.

Even though I haven't, I give Tony a smug look, especially since Frankie stood up for me. Giving me the evil eye, Tony pulls a pipe out of his pocket and holds it up high.

"Bet you never *smoked* it before," he says.

Shrugging, I say proudly, "No, only snorted it. Only the crackheads smoke it."

"Fuck that. You don't know nothin'," Angel says. "Where's the baking soda?"

"How we gonna make any money if you guys keep using the shit?" Frankie yells, pounding his fist on the counter. The blender shakes, and I try not to look nervous, even though it's dangerously close to falling.

Then Frankie laughs and says to me, "I'd complain, but who'd listen?"

Paul says, "Frankie, that's the *cops* who said that in the movie!"

So Frankie smacks him on the head, leaving white cocaine fingerprints in his hair. "It's just a fucking *movie*," he says. "Why don't you shut the fuck up?"

Tony locates the baking soda in the fridge,

and Angel finds a spoon and a saucer. While Tony concentrates on turning some coke into rocks of crack, Frankie cuts the rest of the coke with some other kind of white powdery shit in the blender.

When I finally get to take a hit from the pipe, my head practically explodes.

Cackling like a fucking crazy dude, I go, "What's the point of making money from it if you can't enjoy it too?"

Frankie high-fives me.

Chapter Nineteen

When I got home, it was almost seven. Ma had a pot of stew simmering on the stove. I smelled carrots and onions. Sitting at the kitchen table, Pop made slurping noises as he sucked a small piece of meat off his spoon. With his free hand, he mopped up sauce with a piece of limp white bread.

"Hi, sweetheart," Ma said. I hadn't seen her smile since Mickey left, and we'd eaten frozen dinners from the microwave all last week. Now, suddenly, she was happy. Was Mickey home?

"Should I fix you a plate?" Ma said.

"I'm not really hungry," I said, which was true. I could still taste cocaine in the back of my mouth, and the thick stew smell made me feel a little sick, even though my stomach was growling.

"I'll leave it here on the stove," Ma said, "and you can serve yourself later."

Whoa, I thought. That proved it—something was up around here. Ma never let people choose their own dinnertimes when she was home. Family dinners were very important to her, especially in the past month since she'd started working late and was hardly ever home for dinner.

I ran upstairs and through the bathroom between Mickey's old room and mine. A sloppy pile of belongings slumped on his bed, and I saw tousled curls behind the mess.

"Mickey?" I said, approaching the bed and starting to lean over the crap on it to see if the hair I saw was really attached to his head. I guess I must have missed him more than I thought.

Mickey popped up like a jack-in-the-box, making me jump.

"You ever hear of knocking?" he yelled.

I stepped back, away from the bed. What the fuck was his problem?

"Get outta my room!" Mickey screeched. "Jesus Christ! I'm not back a half hour, and already you're bugging me!"

"I just wanted to say hello," I said.

"Well, say it later, I'm busy right now."

Ma yelled from downstairs, "Mickey, stew's ready!"

Mickey rolled his eyes. "Do me a favor, Catherine, tell Ma to quit bugging me about that fucking stew. I'll eat when I get hungry!"

Now I was mad. "First off," I said, "I'm not your messenger. And another thing, Ma went to the trouble to make you dinner, you better eat it! She's been crying all week. I'd appreciate if you don't make her cry again! Where the hell were you anyway? I didn't see you around the neighborhood. Where did you stay? What the fuck are you doing back?"

"Just get outta my room," Mickey said. "I said, I'm *busy*!"

Instead of heading back to my room through the bathroom, I stomped toward the hallway door, hoping to see what Mickey was hiding behind his bed. As I peeked down, Mickey moved, blocking my view, almost. I *thought* I saw the reflection from a mirror. I looked at Mickey's face, hoping to see a clue there—was he really dealing drugs, like Erica thought she heard? Mickey glared at me, and I left his room.

In my own room, I sat on the edge of my bed, my head hanging. All of a sudden I felt exhausted, and hungry. But I didn't want to go down to the kitchen for stew. After seeing the way Mickey was acting, I couldn't stand to see Ma smiling and hear her humming. She was setting herself up to be hurt. Mickey was worse than ever.

There was a knock on my door. When I didn't answer, it opened a crack. Mickey's fat nose poked in.

"What do you want?" I said, wiping my eye. No way was Mickey going to see me cry, the bastard.

He closed the door gently behind him and sat down on the floor with an ashtray and a cigarette. Without him even offering me one, I took the pack from his hand and got a cigarette for myself.

"I didn't mean to yell like that, Cat, it's just that I'm eighteen and I need some privacy. You can't go barging in like when we were kids."

I noticed a thin red scar near Mickey's ear, and scabby circles on his knuckles. "Better be careful that doesn't get infected," I said. "Want me to get some Neosporin?"

"Naah," Mickey said, "it ain't nothin'. So, what's up with you and Joey? I saw you guys at Snakepit last Saturday. I was gonna say hi, but you and Joey looked so *cozy* together." Mickey grinned.

"For your information, I'm *working* there now," I said. "But you wouldn't understand about working, at an honest, *real* job, would you?"

Mickey was quiet at first; then he grinned nastily again. "What happened to your cafe or whatever shit job uptown?"

I didn't want to know if he knew about

Gatto's. I didn't even want to think about Gatto's—it was part of another life, the sorry life that didn't include Joey's blue eyes.

"How'd your hands get so beat up?" I asked, trying to change the subject. "Ma know you been fighting?"

"Ma know you was out at Snakepit half the night? How come you wasn't working?" Mickey said. He put his battered hand under his folded leg.

"You been hanging out with Frankie?" I asked. "He's bad news, you know. You do know that, don't you? And stop talking like a hood."

"By the way, your friend Erica looked cute in that outfit."

"Mickey, are you in trouble? Why'd you come back home?"

Mickey leaned forward as he put out his cigarette. His blue eyes looked fiercer than I remembered. "I told you I didn't want you hanging out with Joey Valentino," he said.

"What're you, my father?" I said.

"Let me finish," Mickey said. "Turns out, I don't think Joey's such a bad guy. But I still don't think it's a good idea for you—"

I started to say something, but Mickey held up his hand to stop me.

"How*ever*," he continued, "you better be careful. That guy Sally, on the other hand, maybe you should stay away from—"

Then Ma came up the stairs and opened my bedroom door. "Catherine! Sit down at the table and eat your dinner."

She turned around too quickly for me to argue and went into her bedroom and slammed the door behind her. Mickey grinned at me as he ran downstairs and went out the front. I made fists with my hands, then ran down to the kitchen and peeked through the window. Mickey swaggered in his best wannabe mobster persona. Halfway up the block, in front of Benito's, he stopped. From the other direction came Frankie and his crew, swaying in time to invisible music. Mickey didn't wave to them or anything, but after they passed, Mickey's backpack was gone, and he was leaning against the stairway next to Benito's, smoking a butt.

I dumped some stew into a bowl and pulled a slice of bread from the loaf that had been left open on the counter. I got a Pepsi from the refrigerator.

The thing that really sucked was that I couldn't ask Mickey if he *was* dealing cocaine. Not when I was *doing* coke! Especially not since

I *liked* coke and didn't really see anything wrong with it, so long as it was used properly, and carefully, and only for special occasions. But I knew Mickey was different than me. I wasn't so sure he could handle it. Especially the money, and the power that went along with dealing, even if he wasn't using. He'd end up never leaving the neighborhood, except to go to jail.

The stew tasted salty. I licked sauce slowly from my spoon, thinking. When Mickey came in, I pretended not to notice him.

"Hey," he said.

I nodded.

Before filling a bowl of stew for himself, he ruffled my hair. "Don't look so worried," he said. "I know what I'm doing. I ain't in trouble, and I'm working. Soon as I get enough for a new car, I'm gonna start saving to go back to school."

I shrugged. "What kinda car?" I said. I was sick of giving advice he wouldn't hear.

"I haven't decided yet," he said, getting excited. "But Frankie's second cousin has a lot out in Brooklyn, and I was thinking of going out there maybe next week and taking a look. Wanna come?"

"Me?" I said.

Mickey punched me lightly in the arm and smiled. "Shit, if you can get someone like Joey Valentino to take you out, you must be classy! So maybe you could help me pick out the right color and stuff."

I shrugged and concentrated on my stew. I hated to admit it, but it sounded like fun, picking out a car together.

"Is it me, or is this stew kinda salty?" Mickey asked.

Giggling, I whispered, "Shhh! Ma will hear! It is kinda gross, isn't it?"

Mickey reached into his pocket and pulled out a crumpled ten-dollar bill. He took my bowl and his and dumped our stew back in the pot. Turning off the burner, he said, "Let's go down to Canal and get some sweet-and-sour soup and fried rice. My treat."

It was a little weird to be going out together, after all the fights we'd been having lately. Although I was thankful to be friends again, I still wondered where the ten dollars came from, and where the money for his new car was coming from. I also wondered whether I was betraying Ma and Pop by not saying what I'd heard about Mickey. But, I thought, maybe it was nothing. There was no point in worrying Ma if Mickey wasn't doing anything wrong. Anyway, I was too old to be a tattletale. Hopefully, Mickey was too old too, because I didn't want to think what would happen if Ma or Pop found out I'd been to Snakepit with Joey.

Chapter Twenty

"You got any room left in your bag?" Erica asked from the next stall in the Penn Station bathroom. "I can't get my sweatshirt into mine."

"Yeah, just a second," I said. I was sitting on the edge of the toilet seat, pulling on my hooker boots so fast, my pinky toe got caught at an odd angle in the pointed toe of one boot.

"Are you almost ready?" I asked. "We don't want to be late."

Erica passed me her sweatshirt under the stall, and I stuffed it into my backpack, which looked almost ready to burst at the seams. Standing up, I pulled my skirt straight and fluffed my hair with my fingers to make it look bigger, like when a cat bristles its fur in the face of danger.

"We wouldn't be running late if loverboy Joey had driven us to work," Erica said.

"He's not my chauffeur," I said. "Be grateful he got us jobs!"

"Can I borrow your lipstick?" Erica asked.

By catching a cab outside Penn Station, we made it to work on time. Although Snakepit was close enough to walk, we probably would've been arrested by the cops for prostitution, the way we looked. I moped as we picked up our aprons and cigarette boxes. The next day was the SATs, and I hadn't wanted to work that night.

I scanned the rooms as I worked, looking for Joey. He'd said he'd be there that night, and he'd promised he'd try to get me off work early. Erica was having fun and making better tips than me, probably because she was so damn happy. Several trips to the bathroom to attack her cocaine stash didn't hurt either.

Finally, at eleven-thirty, when Joey still hadn't shown, I decided that if I was going to be up, working, until three in the morning, I might as well start having fun. Obviously the SATs were blown now anyway. The next time someone offered to buy me a drink, I asked for a beer and a shot of tequila. At midnight I went on break for a half hour, and after forcing myself through several crowds of giggling women and leering dorks, I found Erica dancing on a table in one of the corner rooms. I got her down and led her to the bathroom.

"Can I have my share of that stuff you got from Sally?" I asked.

Erica shrugged and dug one hand between her breasts, through the neckline of her shirt. She kept her stash in her bra. "I already separated it for you," she said. "I had a feeling you'd want it."

I did two huge lines and leaned back against the sink, feeling my heart beat. The rhythm seemed to travel from my hips to the top of my head. As the first taste of coke rose in my throat, I gagged, but by holding my nose and coughing, I was able to make the nausea go away.

Work got better then, for about an hour. The wannabes didn't bother me so much, and I was able to flirt with the men for tips and buddy up with the girls. After my second shot of tequila, I swaggered up to the deejay booth and introduced myself. The guy in the booth was Denny, and he looked totally out of place. If I weren't already spoken for, I thought, I'd go home with you! He was a total bad boy, with long, uneven, bleached hair, leather pants, motorcycle boots— better keep Erica away from this dude—and rough, bristly hair on his chin.

"Good to meet you," he said. "What's your pleasure?"

I asked if he had any Melissa Etheridge, and I gave him five dollars.

He gave me a thumbs-up and blew a kiss to me as I descended back into the club. I practically melted with sudden lust and wondered where the fuck Joey was. Before I got halfway across the floor, "Like the Way I Do" was playing. Erica and I practically collided in the middle of the dance floor, trying to dance with big boxes of cigarettes hanging from our necks and jutting out two feet from our waists.

Next guy who bought me a drink, I told him to go and tip the deejay and tell him Cat says hi. By the last half hour, Denny was playing Melissa every ten minutes. One thing I'd learned living in my neighborhood—favors made life more livable.

*O*n the way home in the cab, I let Erica handle the driver with directions and stuff. I was stuck between wasted and mad as hell, and I couldn't see straight enough to read the street signs. Keeping one hand flat against my abdomen so I wouldn't feel sick, I stared at the back of the cabdriver's seat. There was a dull aching coming from the back of my skull and wrapping around to my ears, which were still throbbing from the loud music at the club. My hands smelled like cigarette smoke, and there was thick, gray dirt under my nails. My cheeks and jaw ached from smiling, my nose burned from snorting and I had to pee.

Fucking Joey, I thought. He promised! Because of him, not only wasn't I going to get any sleep, but also, I was going to be hung over for my SATs. Thank God I got 1100 the first time, so I could afford to blow it the next day.

"It was a totally different scene this week, wasn't it?" Erica said. I wondered how the hell she could sound so sober and upbeat.

"I guess," I said.

Erica nudged me in the ribs, making me burp. "You know what I mean," she said. "Like last week, everyone stepped aside for us and stuff. This week, it was like we were nobody. Although, I have to say, the girls with their poufy hair and bad eye makeup treated me better. You think they thought we were one of them?"

"Weren't we?" I said, lighting a cigarette, despite the NO SMOKING sign.

"Get real!" Erica said. "What's wrong with you? Just because Joey didn't show up is no reason to act like an idiot, you know. Jeez, Cat, how could we be like those chicks? Would you go on a date with one of those greasy loser wannabe buttheads? Get serious."

I shrugged and didn't talk anymore, except to mumble good night when we were dropped off on Mulberry Street. Fucking Joey, I thought as I went upstairs. I didn't bother to be quiet, because I didn't care if I got caught. It would be a relief. If Ma grounded me for a month, my life would be simpler.

In my room, I crumpled into the corner and slid the boots off my sweaty feet. I unhooked my bra and pulled it off through the sleeves of my blouse. Crawling to the bed, I realized that I didn't want to get in it. Instead, I lay on the coarse carpet, half under the bed. The tassel from my bedspread brushed against my face, bisecting me. When it started to tickle, I flipped onto my stomach and stared at the dust bunnies under the bed. My feet bounced lightly up and down against the floor. Suddenly my stomach cramped, and I rolled out from under the bed, then curled up on my side. When bile rose into my throat, I hurried, bent over and clutching my stomach, into the bathroom. Cloudy swirls of beer and tequila filled the toilet. I climbed into the bathtub and tried to feel the coolness of the porcelain all the way through my body, even inside, soothing my organs.

Pressing my hands against my eyes, I thought, *I want!* It didn't matter what—I wanted everything, and nothing at once. As I started hitting my palms against my cheeks, head, eyes, chest and knees, the voice in my head shouted louder, *"I want! I want! I want!"* until, eventually, it wasn't in my head anymore. First I was whispering it, like a mantra, then I was sobbing it.

Finally the voice stopped, and I felt very tired, but thankfully, not so scared or needy anymore. I stood up carefully in the tub, holding the wall for support as I stepped gently out and went back to my own room. Still feeling a little sick to my stomach, I curled my knees under me to sleep, with my forehead pressed flat against the pillow.

Chapter Twenty-One

I fell asleep during the SATs. When I woke up, I saw that I had filled in an entire column of little circles, and I had to erase them and go back. Somehow I finished the test in time, without throwing up, despite the twisting in my stomach.

Before meeting Erica for work, I did a line, even though I felt like shit, and the coke didn't help. I hadn't eaten since early the day before, and I didn't feel like ever eating again. The smell of food made me want to puke.

On the subway I dug my nails into my arm to keep from bugging out. My breath was fast and shallow. Normally cocaine would make me chatty, but tonight all I could do was smile and nod while Erica blabbered next to me on the crowded train.

We changed our clothes in the bathroom at Penn Station again, and I did another line, even though it was not what I needed. I needed sleep, food and maybe a hug. While Erica bought a hot dog at Nathan's, I paced and gulped air.

My skin prickled every time I had to brush against someone at Snakepit, which was every couple of seconds. I saw some familiar faces from the night before, including a couple of guys who bought me drinks. But their faces blended together above a mushy haze of open shirts and hairy-to-bald chests. I wanted to quit, but, I thought, I need the money. I wondered why I felt so lousy—I was at the height of my partying years. Everyone got wasted all the time in high school. I should be able to binge for days without feeling sick and lonely.

"Cathy," I heard, and felt a dry kiss against the back of my neck.

"I missed you last night," I said as I turned around to smile at Joey. I'd originally thought I'd yell at him, but what would I say?

"Sorry," he said, without looking too con-cerned. "Take a break and come sit with me."

So I did. It was easy. Hanging on to Joey's arm, I didn't feel so scared of myself. Although my stomach still rumbled, I felt like I had some control. The dancing guys and girls parted for us, and suddenly I knew who I was. I wasn't posing to attract some big-time gangster, I *was*

Joey Valentino's girl, even if it was for this moment only.

On the way to the bar Joey said, "Have you
seen Sally tonight?"

"I don't think so."

"What about last night?"

"I don't know," I said, worrying a little.
God, I hoped he didn't know about Sally, me,
Erica and cocaine. He didn't, did he?

"What about Ron—he around?" Joey asked,
looking at me in an oddly intense way.

"What is this, an interrogation?" I said,
laughing and trying to stop the quiz. Until he
tongue-kisses me, I thought briefly, he has no
right to ask me so many questions—he'll tire
out his lips!

Joey laughed.

I put my cigarette case on the bar and leaned
against Joey. Trying not to let my hands shake, I
took a cigarette from the pack he offered and
smoked quietly. I vowed not to do any more
coke tonight, so I could enjoy this feeling of
belonging. Looking up at the deejay booth, I
waved, even though I couldn't see Denny
through the tinted glass. He must've seen me,
though, because Melissa Etheridge's "Chrome-
plated Heart" was the next song played. I gave a
thumbs-up to the booth.

"Could I have ten dollars?" I asked Joey. "I want to tip the deejay."

"You know him?" Joey asked.

I hoped he was feeling jealous. Then maybe he wouldn't leave me alone for a whole night again.

I shrugged. "Kinda. He's a cool guy, and he plays good music."

Joey gave me two fives. I slid off my stool and headed for the booth. I started with my head down and hands in front of me to push my way through the sweaty bodies, but they parted for me, like before. I lifted my chin high and felt great.

"You friends with that poseur?" Denny said, after pecking me on the cheek for the tip I gave him.

"What poseur?" I asked.

Denny gestured toward the bar and Joey.

Angry, I said, "Joey's not a poseur, not like the rest of the people here."

Denny shrugged. "Okay," he said. "Whatever. You like Van Halen?"

I nodded and hurried back to the bar. On the way, I noticed a familiar group heading toward a table in the back. Even as the crowd engulfed them, Mickey's curly hair was unmistakable. So was Frankie's belly, which wobbled from side to side as he strutted. He raised a pudgy hand at Joey as he passed, and Joey nodded so slightly, you wouldn't have noticed it if you weren't looking closely.

"Your brother's here," Joey said as I sat down.

"So?"

"You want me to buy his friends a round?" he said.

I almost said no, but then I thought Frankie needed to be put in his place. He needed to know he wasn't going to play games with *my* brother without me having something to say about it. And furthermore, I didn't want anymore spitballs shot at me in school, or giggling from the gang of long-nailed, big-haired girls Frankie's crew dated.

I helped Joey carry beers and shots to Frankie's table. When I winked at Mickey he smiled, genuinely proud.

"Hey, Cat, how are ya! I didn't know you was working here!" Mickey lied. "Guys, do you know my sister? This is Catherine. Joey, my man! Whassup?"

Joey smiled softly, making me believe that he actually gave a damn about Mickey. I was surprised. Although I knew Mickey had run some errands for Joey, I thought that was over. Maybe

Joey just liked Mickey because he was my family.

"Ain't I seen you around school?" Frankie said to me. "Yeah, I think I have. You're friends with that other girl, the one with the cool boots. My girlfriend's having a party next Friday night, maybe you wanna go? I know she wouldn't mind."

"I'm working," I said, hooking my arm around Joey's elbow.

"Oh yeah, well, maybe another time." Frankie's chubby cheeks were turning pinker the longer I stared at him.

"Guess you don't wanna sit for a drink or somethin', huh, Joey?" said Frankie's second-in-command. "Hey, assholes, why doncha get up and let Joey and his girl sit!"

Two of the musclebound guys with little heads and crew cuts started to squeeze out of their seats, but Joey waved at them to stay. Staring hard at Frankie, he turned quietly, and we slowly walked toward the bar.

"That was so *cool*!" I heard behind me.

"He works for *my* uncle, you know," Frankie was saying. "It ain't such a big deal."

"That's really your sister, Mick? She's hot."

"Lay off," Mickey said.

When Joey and I got back to the bar, I put

154

my box of cigarettes back over my neck. Even though Joey probably could've made sure I didn't have to work the rest of the night, I didn't want the other cigarette girls to get pissed. Anyway, I had to earn some money. I didn't know Joey well enough to ask *him* to pay for my computer, and even if I had known him better, I wasn't a whore.

As I moved back into the crowd, I peeked over the tops of people's heads toward Frankie's table. I caught Mickey staring in my direction, and I felt a warm feeling spreading through my body. Finally, Mickey was proud. Now maybe he'd listen to me.

Chapter Twenty-Two

Miller's Crossing is mostly about some kind of Irish mob, but I like the movie anyway. I'm watching it on Sunday afternoon, down in the living room because no one's home, and I'm feeling okay, so I don't even get pissed off that the Italian dude in the movie is made out to be stupid.

I pause the movie for a second, right when the cool Irish guy, Tommy, cracks a thug over the head with a fucking chair. Running upstairs, I go under the bed for the shit Sally gave me last week to weigh and package, and I do a big fat line. It's not as good as smoking, but I can't do that shit in my mother's house, you know? I wish I was still at Joey's, but I'm doing so much work here in the city, I can't deal with that long commute from Brooklyn. Fuckin' A, not with the shit I'm carrying.

I'm buzzing when Ma comes home. She asks, real fucking bitchy-like, if I'm staying for dinner.

I go, "Hold on, Ma, this is a good part."

So she turns off the VCR, the screen goes

fuzzy and she says, "Don't get high-hatted with me, young man!"

Casper, the dumb Italian in the movie, is always bitching about people giving him the "high hat," so what can I do? I gotta crack up. Ma doesn't understand—she never does—and I'm laughing so hard, I'm like ready to pee in my pants. I'm thinking my heart's going to burst from all the coke and laughing, so I try to stop, which makes my eyes water.

Ma grabs me by the ear and pulls me toward the kitchen. If she thinks she's going to swat me with the wooden spoon, she better think again. Already I'm eyeing the kitchen chair as a weapon. Goddamn, she's got some long fucking fingernails! Thanks, Ma, I'm thinking even while I'm still giggling, I always wanted my ear pierced.

Twist a pig's ear, watch him squeal, is what Leo says in the movie. Fuck that. I ain't crying.

Suddenly Ma's stuck my head in the kitchen sink, and cold water is splashing all over. I jerk up so fast, I hit my head on the tap, and then Ma pushes my head down again, and I bang my ear. Always put one in the brain, Ma. Jesus Christ! Practically puking from the taste of beer rising in my throat, I try again and this time get free. I shake water out of my hair like a dog.

"What the fuck are you doing?" I say.

Ma is pulling on her hair, like she does when she's really mad. I hear Catherine come in and pretend to go upstairs, so now I know, after dealing with Ma, I'm going to have to deal with her too!

Ma goes, "Are you high?"

"No, Ma, I'm not fucking high."

She slaps me, and I grab her wrist before she can take another swing.

But I just say, "I'm not high, okay? God, why do you always think I'm doing something wrong? How come you never ask Catherine if *she's* high? Jesus Christ, you don't go turning off *her* movies right in the middle! You don't dunk *her* head in the sink!"

"We're not talking about your sister," Ma says. I hear a step creak, so I know Catherine's trying to sneak away.

"Of course not," I say. "We never do. Let's talk to Catherine now. Cat! Ma wants to know where you've been all day!"

Then I stare hard at Ma and go, "That's what you're always asking me, where I've been. Ask *her* for a change."

There's no sound from the stairs, and Ma

changes the subject, as usual. "I don't like those new friends of yours. Frankie and those guys are nothing but deadbeats and trouble. I want you to stay away from them."

"Friends is a mental state," I say, like Casper.

I wish I had another hit, or a line, or something, *anything* to get me through this stupid fucking conversation. Especially since Frankie's practically ancient history. I work for Sally now. I'm in the big time, Ma! Only I can't tell her that. She's so fucking close-minded. I wonder if Cat would get it?

Without even thinking about it, I start walking away, and Ma doesn't follow me. I see Cat going into her room as I head up the stairs, so I give her the finger. But then I feel guilty, so as I'm bracing the bathroom door between our rooms shut with a chair, I blow a kiss in her direction.

Later I re-count all the grams I packaged, which I'm supposed to deliver to Snakepit for Sally in a half hour. Then I count them *again,* and I'm now starting to sweat. I cut the shit as much as I could, and I skimped on the weight as much as I could, but fuckin' A, goddamn it! There's still only sixteen bags, which means Ron at the Pit is going to pay me practically three hundred dollars less than I'm supposed to pay

Sally on Friday. Fuckin' A! I mean, I fucking thought I only used like a gram for myself, but I mean, it's real fucking stressful living in this house, you know? But Sally wouldn't go for that. I already owe him a hundred. At first I think I'll just cut some of the coke a little more, only I keep thinking of Ron's big goons and what'll happen if I deliver crap tonight. *I'll* be headed for Miller's Crossing.

So I bring Ron the sixteen grams, and he pays me thirteen hundred bucks, and I head for the back door wondering where I can get some quick cash to make up the difference for Sally. As I'm going out, I bump into someone coming in.

"Joey! Hey, man, good to see you! That was cool, you buying the guys drinks last night! It's cool you got my sister that job . . ."

Joey grabs me by the arm with a fucking killer grip and whispers, "What're you doing here?"

I'm like, "What—my sister send you to spy on me? What're *you* doin' here? And how've you been, anyway? Cat's—"

Joey pulls me outside and says, "I'm only going to tell you this once. Stay away from here.

160

You don't want to be here this week. Don't tell me what you're doing—I don't want to know. But if you're really as smart as your sister says you are, you'll quit doing it, whatever it is."

Man, the dude's freaking out, I think, and I say, "Hey, Joey, I'm not trying to move in on your—"

"I don't want to hear it. Stop talking. I'm doing you a favor. Go home."

Shrugging, I go, "Yeah, whatever. It's cool. See you around, Joey."

As I walk away, confused, I remember Sally's money and smack myself on the head. Why didn't I ask Joey for a fucking loan? He's so fucking into being my guardian fucking angel, he should put his money where his mouth is!

Chapter Twenty-Three

The cab slowed almost to a stop about a block away from Snakepit, the traffic was so bad. I looked at my watch. It was almost nine, so Erica and I got out to walk.

"Wonder what's up?" she said. "What's with the flashing lights? Think somebody's hurt?"

Oh God, I thought, I hope it's not someone I know. Even though it was early and Snakepit would still be somewhat empty, the wannabes always drank before showing up at the club. The early hours were the most dangerous for fights, because the cliques and gangs were sparse enough that they could all see each other across the dance floor. There was always a lot of posing before eleven, and a lot of angry looks. Guys and girls both stuck their chests out too far, and all it took was for someone's girl to bump into someone else's girl on line at one of the bathrooms, or one guy's bodyguard spilling his drink on the wrong end of the bar, for a fight to get started.

But usually the bouncers kept everything

cool before anything happened. There were even metal detectors at the front door so no one could bring weapons in. Erica and I walked more slowly as we got closer and saw that the flashing lights were definitely in front of Snakepit.

But it wasn't an ambulance, it was a line of police cars that curved all the way around the corner. Some customers were being led out with their hands clasped behind their heads while their friends clustered as close as they could, yelling support and cursing at the cops, who pushed them away like you'd push your vegetables to the edge of your plate.

Erica and I hung back while the owner, the older guy who was Joey's friend, was led outside by two policemen. They let him lock the door, and then they stuffed him into the last car in the long row. One by one the cars pulled away.

A bunch of men in suits were standing on the curb, ignoring the crowd of curious passersby, who were already beginning to move on, and talking to some of the daytime cigarette girls and bartenders. Erica and I carefully edged closer.

"What's going on?" I asked one of the girls.

"Busted," she said. "Drugs, I think."

"So they're closed down for the night?" Erica asked.

"*Duh!*" the girl said, and I wanted to punch her for being snotty to us. Maybe I'll tell my boyfriend about you, you little bitch, I thought.

"Might not open again for a while," one of the plainclothes cops said. I hadn't noticed him. "Mind if I ask you a few questions?"

"Questions?" Erica said. "Why ask us? We were just passing by. Just curious, that's all." Grabbing my elbow, she said to me, "Come on, Jo, let's not bother these people."

"Okay, Alison," I said, trying not to crack up, even though Erica was being totally serious. What'd she think this was, *Cops* or something? Now I was sure we'd been living in Little Italy, with all the gangster wannabes talking like they were in a bad TV show, for too long.

Still, I really didn't want to talk to the police, especially not with half a gram of cocaine in my bra. Erica and I walked briskly to Seventh Avenue and hailed a cab.

"So what do you think we should do tonight?" I asked. "I don't feel like going home. Mickey's in trouble again. Do you think Joey was involved in that?"

"Naah," Erica said. "I don't think Joey's into

164

the drug thing, do you? Anyway, he's not the type to get caught."

"I hope not. I'm kind of worried."

"I know how we could find out, and have something to do, too," Erica said, snapping her fingers. I wished I could snap like that—loud and sharp, like a small gun firing.

*N*ext thing I knew, we were stopping on Mott Street and Canal. I, who had always said I wouldn't pay for drugs, was not only clutching two crumpled tens in a sweaty fist, but also was going with Erica to Sally's apartment. Not the one where he lived, which was down in Bensonhurst, but the one where he sold dope to his Manhattan customers. Even though I'd given money to Erica before, it was different to be going into the drug den myself. What if we got busted?

"Quit worrying," Erica said. "It's easy. I call from the pay phone on the corner to be sure he's there, then we go to his building, and I use my key to get in. We press the buzzer outside his door, which doesn't buzz, it just lights up inside, Sally lets us in, and we're gone in two minutes, unless you want to party there?"

I shook my head and concentrated on my

breathing while Erica dialed Sally's number, which, apparently, she knew by heart. I thought of what I'd say if cops stopped us after we'd been inside. I'd say I cleaned his apartment on weekends and was just picking up my pay. No, I'd say I was delivering some mail that had been incorrectly sent to my house. Maybe I'd just run.

I kept my eyes facing front as we walked around the corner to Sally's place. I figured if I didn't see anybody, they wouldn't see me and tell Ma or Pop they saw me in hooker boots and a miniskirt, walking on Mott Street after dark.

Sally answered the door in his underwear, and I blushed. Before we'd even shut the door behind us, he plopped back down on the couch, where he'd evidently been for a while, by the looks of the surrounding floor. Two six-packs of beer cans were scattered around the edge of the couch, mingled with several bags of chips and a half-finished plastic container of onion dip. A mangy-looking German shepherd was licking the cap from the dip container. Erica patted the dog.

"Stuff's on the table. Put the money in the drawer," Sally said.

"You want a line?" Erica asked.

"Naah, I'm cutting down," Sally said. He patted the sagging skin that hung from his ribs over the waist of his underwear.

"Do you mind?" Erica said, as she sat at the small Formica table and dumped some coke out.

Sally shrugged, and Erica started cutting us two lines. I had to admit, I felt pretty cool to be hanging out in a big dealer's apartment, getting ready to do a line on his kitchen table—even if the place was starting to give me a headache, it smelled so bad. There weren't any windows.

After snorting a line, I had enough courage to say, "Have you heard from Joey?"

Sally looked up from the TV. He rubbed a pockmarked cheek with one hand, as if I'd asked him a difficult question. Then he said, "I hear from him sometimes. Why do you ask?"

Christ! Did I look like a cop or something? "I was just worried," I said. "There was some kind of trouble at Snakepit tonight, and I was hoping Joey was okay."

That woke Sally up, big-time. Suddenly he was pulling on pants so fast, he could hardly get his foot through. He splashed water on his face at the sink.

"Sorry, girls, I got business. You gotta go now. When did this happen? At the Pit, I mean."

As we were being practically shoved out the door, I said, "Right before nine. So you don't know anything about Joey?"

"Why don't you call him yourself and ask him?" Sally said in a tone I thought was a little snotty, considering I was Joey's girlfriend and all.

*E*rica asked me the same thing much later, when we were sitting in her room about midnight, sipping blackberry brandy out of coffee mugs. I was wearing a pair of her jeans, rolled up, and fastened to my waist with a belt that made the canvas bunch out around my hips like a paper bag filled with air. I'd called my mother earlier to say I'd finished work early and was sleeping over at Erica's. Ma had only grunted before hanging up. I guessed she hadn't settled things with Mickey yet.

"Come on," Erica said, "we can call from the kitchen. My mother's probably asleep in her Cheez Doodles by now, and my father's not even home yet. We can call from the kitchen, if you talk quiet. Maybe Joey'll know a cool place we can go hang out!"

"I don't really feel like going out," I said. I felt so tweaked, I didn't think I could survive in a bar or a club full of people.

"Why don't you want to call Joey? You afraid he's with another girl?"

Actually, that hadn't crossed my mind until Erica said it. "Thanks a lot," I said.

"Call him already!" Erica said. "Christ, do you want to be waiting around for him all the time? I mean, he's cool, but you have a life too, right?"

I hadn't been so sure of that, these past few weeks. I didn't know if it was the coke, or trying to impress Joey, or suddenly being popular with the Guido-chicks at school, or maybe just that Mickey was out of control. Somehow, a few months earlier, in August, I'd known who I was. Now, with November and the due date for college applications coming on quick, I didn't even know what I *wanted* to be.

"You know his number, don't you?" Erica said, picking fuzz off a pink rabbit with a leather Harley cap that sat on her pillow.

I flattened a wrinkle in the white woven bedspread. "It's just that Joey told me his phone was for business and he couldn't use it for social chatting."

"You're not going to *chat*, just say, 'Hey, what's up, wanna do something?' " Erica said.

I got up. "Let's go then," I said.

After eight rings Joey answered the phone in a groggy voice, but still sounding curt, like I'd heard him talk to his business associates. I didn't say anything but hung up fast, suddenly afraid of making him angry so he wouldn't want to see me anymore. I felt like a jerk for calling, *and* for hanging up.

It was just as well we didn't go out, because an hour later, Erica was passed out on top of her covers. I shut the light off so she could sleep and sat at the edge of the bed, after doing a line from my private stash. I liked the way crumbs of the coke glistened in the moon-light that sliced through the crack in the cur-tains.

I knew there was no way I'd sleep. I felt like a cliché—you always hear about coke fiends being "shivering wrecks," and that's what I was. I couldn't even lie down, I was so wired. When I tried to relax, my hands jerked back and forth, uncontrollably spasming.

I heard Erica's father come in and thought of asking him to take me to the hospital, in case I was OD'ing, but when I heard the muffled crack of his hand against Erica's mother's doughy flesh, I decided to stay put. Anyway, I'd always been sure my destiny was to die in my sleep. So long as I stayed awake, which wasn't a problem, I'd be fine. If I felt really bad, I'd wake up Erica.

As I chopped another line, I thought, This isn't getting me anywhere. I had to reroll a dollar three times because my hands were shaking so badly and I kept screwing up and rolling it too loosely. I thought, This is not the way to get out of this neighborhood. I didn't want to find myself hanging around just because my dealer lived three blocks away. I certainly didn't want to grow my hair long, pouf it up with hairspray and paint my nails and lips matching shades of pink.

Pulling a sheet of paper from Erica's looseleaf, I thought, If I'm going to be up all night, I might as well do something useful. I planned to start a story, but the words wouldn't come, except in my head. Leaning back against the edge of the bed, I clenched and unclenched my toes, trying to think happy thoughts and tearing the sheet of paper into narrow strips.

My face was hot, and I felt my heartbeat somewhere behind my forehead, instead of in my chest. Pouring myself some more brandy, I started to cry for being so stupid lately.

I wondered where Mickey was tonight.

Chapter Twenty-Four

I tried to call Joey several times the next week. Finally I saw him in the neighborhood almost a week after the Snakepit bust. He was walking up Mulberry Street with his head down, kicking a Coca-Cola can in front of him. He didn't even notice me until I ran up and grabbed his arm.

"Cathy!" he said, his blue eyes opening wide.

"I've missed you," I said. I stood on my tiptoes to kiss him, and he turned his head, so all I got was a stubbly cheek.

"I've been very, very . . . busy," he said, attempting a smile.

"So I guess you wouldn't want to get together this weekend?" Now I was trying not to choke and start crying. From the way he was keeping his distance it was obvious he'd been avoiding me all week. What did I do wrong?

"It's not you," he said, looking up at the gray sky as wind blew his carefully styled hair askew. "But there's things I'm working on now . . . I don't want to get you involved."

I started to back away.

"I *like* you," he said, almost desperately. "And your brother, too—"

"Leave Mickey out of this! God! Can't I have a life of my own for once?"

As I turned and started to walk away, Joey fell into step next to me. I could hear his heels clicking against the pavement, despite the rising spurts of wind.

"Cathy, I know your friend Erica likes him, but take my advice and don't hang around Sally," he said, putting his hand on my shoulder. I shrugged him off.

"You don't even want to see me anymore, and you think you can tell me who I can be friends with?" I yelled.

"You don't understand. It's not that I don't want—"

"Just forget it!" I said, and walked away as fast as I could, cold tears slipping like icicles off my bottom lashes.

So I was feeling pretty awful when I met Erica in the cafeteria that Friday. I'd even been cutting back on the drugs, because, I told myself, Joey wouldn't like it. But I hadn't seen or heard from him for a week since our argument, so that wasn't really it. I also told myself that all that coke was depleting my savings, which was true. And then, when I really wanted a line, I'd remind myself that coke made it harder to sleep at night. If I fell asleep in English once more, I was going to get some major detention time, which wouldn't look good on my college applications. But stopping doing coke at night ended up just making me feel stupid when I was still awake until two in the morning. My insomnia was back, full force. My one consolation as I lay awake, twitching and turning—and the thing that sometimes, finally, knocked me out—was that if I did die in my sleep, at least I'd beat Mickey to heaven.

Except I was starting to get tired of beating Mickey at things. That was the real reason, I began to realize, that I didn't want to do coke so much. I was sick of trying to be Mickey, only better. And I was sick of trying to make him feel good so I could feel good. I was sick of his life even more than I was confused about my own. If I wasn't Mickey's sister, then who was I?

So much for integration, I thought as I waited on the hot-lunch line and looked out at the tables. On the left were the Asian kids. On the right were the black kids, most of whom hated the Asians, and vice versa. Down the middle were the Italians, who hated everyone but themselves. They thought everyone else was moving in on their neighborhood, even though most of them weren't even *from* the neighborhood. Those of us who'd grown up here didn't care who moved in, we just wanted to move out.

The only place where there was any real mixing was in the back, where the artists, nerds and other outcasts sat. That was where Erica was, saving a table.

It's not like I *couldn't* be popular, I thought, as I got near the Italian Big Hairs in the center row of tables. It's just I wasn't born with money, and I wouldn't want to waste it on high heels and permanents anyway. Get a life, I thought, as Carla and her plastic-nosed friends looked me over. It wasn't so long ago you were kissing my ass because *I have a life*!

"Hey, Catherine," Carla shouted loud enough for half the cafeteria to hear, "I heard Joey Valentino blew you off because you suck in bed!"

I kept my cool and tried not to blush as another girl shrieked, "Naah, she's still a virgin!"

Yeah, well, I'd rather be a virgin than sleep with your stinky boyfriend! I thought. Anyway, Joey didn't dump me, and you're all just jealous because while you're *wishing* you could date a gangster, I already have!

I didn't say anything out loud because I didn't want to fight. I was tired and hungry and just wanted to get to the back of the cafeteria, sit down and eat my Salisbury steak and mashed potatoes before it got cold.

As it turned out, I didn't have a choice. Someone put out her foot and tripped me, and my tray landed on Carla. I couldn't have done any better if I'd aimed. As gravy dripped from her chin to her cashmere sweater and suede skirt, she tossed her milk at me. The rest of the cafeteria united for a common cause and screamed, "Fight! Fight!"

Carla jumped at me, then howled when she broke a nail against my face. I punched her in the stomach. Next thing I knew, we were waiting outside the vice principal's office. We both got a week's detention, which didn't seem fair, since she'd started it.

"How was school today?" Ma asked at dinner.

For once Mickey was eating with the family. "She got in a fight," he said.

"Shut up!" I said. "God, can't I tell you *anything*? You're a jerk." I wanted to call him something worse, but Ma probably would've washed my mouth out with soap.

"I thought you got that scratch in science class," Ma said.

Mickey smirked. Here I spent all this time trying to keep him out of trouble, and what thanks did I get? He got me *into* trouble! What other secrets had he told, and why did *I* keep lying for *him*?

"You're grounded until the weekend, young lady. Straight home after school, and no TV," Ma said.

"How come Mickey can come home whenever he wants, and do what he wants all day, and you don't ground *him*?" I yelled, slamming the salt shaker on the table for emphasis. "You wouldn't punish *him* for fighting!"

Pop finally looked up from his plate and said in an even, tired voice, "No arguing at the table. For Chrissakes, I'm trying to eat!"

No one talked for the rest of the meal, and I hardly ate. After dinner Pop went into the den and turned on the TV. Mickey put his plate by the sink and went upstairs. I started to follow, but Ma stopped me.

"Help me with the dishes," she said.

"You know," I said as I cleared Pop's plate,

"I'm really sick of this! How come *I* have to help with the dishes?"

"I always helped my mother with the dishes. It's one of the joys of having children," Ma said sarcastically as she passed me a towel.

"How come Mickey doesn't have to help?"

Turning on the water, Ma said without looking at me, "Catherine, your brother is pretty much lost to me. If I asked him to help, he might even laugh in my face. So I don't ask. You're a good girl, Catherine. Can't you just let me enjoy it? One Mickey is enough in this house. Don't defy me. I've got enough to worry about already."

Yeah, don't we all, I thought. But I took the plates as she handed them to me and started drying.

Chapter Twenty-Five

Snakepit was closed for another week. Because I was grounded, I didn't even bother to try calling Joey. I was ready to make up, but what good would it do if I wasn't allowed out anyway? It hurt a little that he didn't call me either, but I figured he knew how my mother would feel about *that*. He was, really, too old for me anyway, and not the type of person a girl like me *should* get too close to. Still, I spent a lot of time looking out the front window, searching for a glimpse of his Mercedes. I missed the way he called me Cathy and the way his long eyelashes fluttered when he was concentrating.

Mickey was hardly part of the family at all anymore. Nights when I couldn't sleep, I'd hear him come in at three or four in the morning. He woke up about the time I came home from school, and always hurried out again before Ma or Pop came home. The few times I saw him were when he was prowling around the neighborhood with Frankie and his crew. Mickey had evidently moved up, because now he walked alongside Frankie.

I noticed Mickey was looking skinny, his hair

was getting long, and he always seemed to have a few days' worth of stubble on his face. If he wasn't careful, I thought, he wouldn't even be able to hang with the top wannabe crowd. He was becoming a bum.

I stopped doing coke for a few days after the night in Erica's room. But then I had two essays to write for my college applications, and I realized I still had a little left in my stash. When that was done, I went to Sally's myself to get a little more. I told myself I was really going to find out what was happening with Joey, but Sally didn't talk about people who weren't there to talk back.

The end of the second week without Joey, I was walking home from school, alone because Erica had to stay late at the yearbook meeting. The trees were already bare, and even though it was only three-thirty, the sky was gray and dim. It made me wonder what it must feel like to go through fall in New England, or someplace where the leaves changed color before dropping dead to the ground.

I decided I wasn't going to let that happen for Joey and me. I wasn't going to let our relationship—if you could call it that, since we'd never even tongue-kissed—die before it could grow and change. I could still recite his phone number in my head. I would call him when I got home.

Ma and Pop were at the kitchen table. Jesus, I thought as I scurried past the doorway, doesn't anybody work in the house? Pretty soon we'll need whatever Mickey's doing for money, just to pay the bills. I noticed that as pissed off as Ma had been about how Mickey was making money, it hadn't stopped her from making scampi for dinner with the three pounds of shrimp he'd brought home the next night.

"Catherine!" Ma said.

I stopped at the foot of the stairs. Damn, I thought I'd made it. I shuffled back to the kitchen and peeked in.

"Sit," Pop said in a gravelly, hoarse voice.

He had a glass in front of him, and his spare bottle of whiskey. Before he could pour himself more, Ma grabbed the bottle and slammed it onto the counter behind her. For a second it looked like he was going to hit her, but she stared him down, and he sank back into his chair and turned his anger to me.

Uh-oh, I thought. What do they know? Mickey didn't tell them anything, did he?

"What do you know about drugs?" Ma said.

I shrugged and wrung my hands in my lap. How could they know?

"Are they easy to get around here?" Pop said. "Who sells? Does that punk Frankie sell drugs?"

I shrugged again.

Ma sighed forcefully, like she was really pissed at me. What did I do?

After several uncomfortable seconds of silence, except for Pop tapping the side of his glass, Ma said, "We found this in your brother's room."

She held up a small pipe. For all my savvy, *I* wasn't even sure what it was. So at least I could answer honestly when she asked.

"I don't believe it's for tobacco," Ma said. "Is it for pot?"

I didn't want to say it, but the more I looked at it, the more I thought it might be a crack pipe. But that didn't *seem* like Mickey. I could imagine him selling dope to make some quick money, and to fit in, but *using? Crack?* Wouldn't I have noticed?

Pop reached behind Ma and retrieved his whiskey. This time she didn't stop him, but instead got a glass of her own. I was embarrassed.

"Your brother doesn't live here anymore," Pop said. I could see that his eyes were watering, probably not just from the booze. I was more embarrassed.

"Mickey moved out again?" I asked.

"A locksmith will be here in a half hour," Pop said, gulping from his glass. His hand was shaking. "Go upstairs and pack a few things your brother might need. Underwear, socks, stuff like that. We'll leave it for him in the foyer."

"Me? Why do I have to do it? This isn't *my* idea!" I said, not only because I didn't want to be involved in throwing Mickey out, which wasn't such a big deal, considering he was eighteen and kept saying he wanted privacy, but also because I didn't want to go through his underwear drawer. Who wants to touch their brother's underwear?

I felt like I was cracking up inside when I started to giggle, and I tried to cover my mouth. I was close enough to Pop for him to swat me good, and Ma was right next to the drawer with the spoon in it. But Ma seemed to understand, for once. She got up and patted me on the shoulder. Then she pressed her cheek against mine. I could feel the slickness of tears between our skin, and I didn't know if they were hers or mine.

"I'll do the packing," Ma said. "Go on and start your homework."

"How's school, anyway?" Pop said, trying

too hard to be cheery. His voice was high and cracked.

I couldn't say anything, so I just shrugged.

Ma put her strong arm over my shoulders and walked with me toward the stairs. I was shaking. It didn't seem fair for me to be treated nicely when Mickey was in so much trouble. Even so, I was relieved.

I didn't want to push my luck, but finally I said anyway, "Maybe we could get the whole family together and have a talk? Before changing the locks, I mean."

"Honey, Mickey isn't part of this family anymore," Ma said. She seemed to be having trouble saying it.

"But it's not true!" I said. "How can you just throw his things outside—"

"Drop it, Catherine. You wouldn't understand."

"But think how he'll feel, when he comes home and—"

My mother stopped at the top of the stairs and grabbed me by the shoulders. Her fingers were strong, and they hurt. Instead of cringing, I glared at her.

"Listen to me, little girl," she said. "Pop and I have *tried* to be here for Mickey. While you've been at your job, and out with your friends until all hours of the morning—yes, I've heard you come in, I'm not an idiot—we've been here, having long 'talks' with your brother. He's threatened your father with a knife. He's high, or drunk, or both, all the time. Maybe if you'd been home more often, we'd have had a family discussion. But it's too late now for any more discussion. I guarantee you, your brother will not be surprised when he comes home tonight. He's had it coming for a long while."

She makes it sound like it's *my* fault, I thought.

Ma softened then and leaned down to hug me. I felt stiff and uncomfortable. I couldn't remember the last time I'd been hugged by Ma. Anyway, I was trying to be mad. If ever I needed a line of cocaine, I needed one now.

"It's okay, Catherine," Ma whispered. "It's for the best, you'll see. It's the only way to reach him."

As she went into Mickey's room, I realized I wasn't going to get to call Joey tonight.

Chapter Twenty-Six

On Tuesday Pop didn't come home from work. Ma tried to pretend she wasn't worried or upset by concentrating on cracking nuts for stuffing. Thanksgiving was only two days away.

At eight o'clock the phone rang. Apparently Pop had left work early and was drunk in a bar in the meat district. I went outside to catch a cab for Ma while she searched her bedroom for Pop's scarf and hat. He always hid them so Ma couldn't make him wear them. He said that when he did, he felt like a little kid bundled up by his mommy.

As Ma got into the cab her shoulders were back and her chin was high. No matter what, I knew she'd always be proud, and strong. Too bad Pop couldn't learn from her. The trouble with Mickey was hurting him badly.

It was hurting me, too, but I didn't want to think about it. I hadn't done any coke since Ma had found Mickey's crack pipe, which I still believed wasn't really his. He must have been holding it for someone else.

I finished my homework at eight-thirty, and Ma and Pop were still out. I wanted to call

Erica, or even Joey, but first I took out my envelope of money and started counting. It always made me feel good.

Bills were scattered in front of me when I heard the buzzer. Someone was pressing it long and hard. It stopped for a minute; then someone started pounding on the door to our apartment—the Fuscos from upstairs must've let someone into the building. I stopped to grab Mickey's old baseball bat from under his bed before hurrying downstairs.

"Who is it?" I yelled from the front hallway.

"Cat, it's me, open up!"

It was Mickey. His words were mushy, like there was something in his mouth.

Leaning the bat against the wall, I said, "I can't. Ma and Pop said you're not allowed in here."

"Cat, I need help, open up!"

"Hold on a second!" I shouted over his pounding against the door. "Quit making so much noise! You want Mrs. Fusco to call the police? I'm coming right out."

I opened the door and gasped. Mickey's eye was swollen, and his lip was puffy and bleeding. No wonder he sounded funny when he tried to talk. His knuckles were scraped, and he held them tightly at his sides. I forgot about Ma and Pop and stepped aside so he could come in.

"What happened?" I asked.

"Nothing," he said.

"Nothing? You come here begging me for help, and you say nothing's the matter?"

Mickey shrugged. "Just a fight with the guys," he said. "It's no big deal. I just need to get cleaned up and pick up a few things. Where is everybody?"

"Is anyone coming after you?" I said as I hurried back to the front door and turned all the locks.

"Why don't you just get me some ice?" Mickey said.

I put some ice cubes in a dishtowel and gave it to him. He held it against his eye for a second and then dumped the ice in the sink and wet the towel.

"You should ice it," I said.

"Forget it, I ain't got time for that shit. I'm fine. It hardly even hurts. We got any Band-Aids?"

I went to the bathroom in Ma and Pop's room and found iodine, cotton balls, Band-Aids and Neosporin. Mickey was sitting at the kitchen table when I returned, mopping blood off his face. He squirmed when I wiped the cut over his eye with iodine, but I made him sit still until I was done bandaging him properly.

"I still think you need some ice," I said.

Suddenly, from the hall, I heard Ma shout, "Catherine! Open the door, my hands are full! Hurry up!"

"Oh shit," Mickey said as he bolted from the kitchen and up the stairs. "Don't say I'm here, okay?"

Bullshit, I thought as I opened the front door and helped Ma drag Pop to bed. I've done enough for you.

"*B*ut Ma, he was *bleeding*!" I argued.

"One simple rule we made, just *one rule*! And you can't even follow that. You are grounded, young lady. For one week."

I was in the kitchen with Ma, handwashing the towel Mickey had bloodied. Typical, I thought. Mickey fucks up, and *I* get grounded! I'd thought Ma would be more understanding, I mean, he was her *son*, for God's sake. Goddamn, how did I get this family? I thought angrily.

A voice from the hallway startled me. I hadn't heard Mickey come downstairs. "What're you grounding *her* for?" he said. "She was just trying to help."

Ma stood up fast. The bowl of nuts on her lap crashed to the floor. "This is not an emergency room," she said. "If the life you chose gets you hurt, you can damn well take care of it yourself. I will not have you bring it home here!"

"Yeah, well, at least I know *somebody* in my family gives a shit what happens to me!" Mickey yelled. "Or maybe you're not my family anymore. Would you like that? You can just have one, good daughter, who will go to college and bring home nice grades, and maybe be a schoolteacher or something."

Mickey sneered at me when he said that, and I wanted to throw the wet towel in his face. How dare he use *me* to make his stupid point? I was sorry I'd let him in.

"Get out of my house before I call the police!" Ma screamed.

Mickey swaggered out. I noticed he'd changed to a clean set of clothes and had filled a bag with some other things.

I couldn't wait for Thanksgiving. We had so fucking much to be thankful for.

Chapter Twenty-Seven

After Mickey left, I went upstairs. Neither Ma nor I said another word to each other, and at the moment, I didn't care if I ever talked to her again.

Slamming the door to my room, I flopped onto my back on my bed. When I'd squeezed back the tears I didn't want to come, I turned my head to the side and practically screamed. The money I'd left scattered on the floor earlier was gone, except for a small stack of singles.

I rolled off the bed and looked under it. Picking up the manila envelope, I shook it. When nothing came out, I ripped it apart, and kept ripping until it was a pile of yellow-orange, violent shreds on the rug.

I pounded my hands against my forehead, trying to feel something—anything—except what I was feeling. I *hated* Mickey. How could he steal from me? After everything I'd done for him? After I'd taken care of him all these years. If he'd only *asked*. But I wasn't sure I'd have given it to him if he had.

I couldn't even tell Ma on him. If I was lucky, she'd tell me she told me so. But more than likely, she'd ask where I got that kind of money in the first place, and why I wasn't putting it into my college fund.

Stomping so hard my soles tingled, I threw myself into Mickey's room and began destroying it. I expected Ma to come upstairs and see if everything was okay, but she didn't. I ripped his clothes off their hangers and pulled down the few posters left on the walls. Under the bed I found Mickey's old baseball card collection and systematically tore each card in half. The more I tore, the less violent I felt, and the sadder.

At ten o'clock I went into the hall and leaned my back against the wall. When I heard the TV in the den go silent and heard Ma close her bedroom door behind her, I slinked into my room to get a sweater, hat and sneakers.

It was starting to snow outside, and the sidewalk was slippery. I walked carefully, with my hat pulled down low. I wasn't just trying to stay warm, I was trying to look like a bad choice for mugging, which I was.

The neighborhood near Sally's place was scary at night, but I was immune to fear. What did I care if someone stabbed me? What did I care if I slipped off the wet sidewalk and was run down by a drunk in a beat-up car? It would make my life simpler to be dead. At least maybe I'd get a headline.

There was a homeless guy sleeping at the base of the phone on Sally's corner. I didn't care. Go ahead, I thought as I leaned over him and dropped a quarter in the slot, go ahead and jump up and slit my throat.

"Sally, can you spot me a half a gram? You know I'm good for it."

"I know you are," Sally said to me, rubbing a hand against his pockmarked cheek, "but I can't go changing policy just because I like someone, you get me?"

"Sally . . ."

He snapped his fingers. "I got it! You could work for me! Yeah, that would solve both our problems. See, I have to go out for about an hour, and, well, come see for yourself."

He led me inside and showed me the scale and two bags of cocaine on the table. It looked like two pounds or something. In a shiny metal bowl were folded white packets of cocaine that had already been weighed. My mouth watered even at the powder that lay in a thin coat of dust over the tabletop.

"Yeah, I know it's a mess," Sally said. "That's my dilemma. I gotta go out, but I can't just leave all this shit all over when I go. On the other hand, it's a bitch to clean up and then take out again, you know? So, how about I give you a whole gram, and while I'm gone, you do some weighing and packaging. I know I can trust you."

Sally glared at me when he said that, and I had a vision of what would happen if I wasn't trustworthy. Taking a deep breath, I finally shrugged, and Sally showed me what to do. Before leaving, he cut us both monster lines out of one of the Baggies.

"On me," he said.

"I can't do that much at once," I whispered.

"Whatever," he said, snorting his, then wiping his nose with the back of his hand. "Am I clean?"

I knocked a stray flake off his upper lip with my fingernail.

"Don't answer the phone. If someone comes to the door, you can look in the TV in here to see who it is. It's hooked up to a camera that shows everything in the hallway. Shouldn't be any problems, though, so don't worry about it. But if you have to get out fast, look . . ."

After showing me the small black-and-white

in the bathroom, he moved the hamper aside. There was a board about eighteen inches square, hinged and flush against the stained wallpaper. When he lifted the board, wind blew small flakes of snow and a stray leaf inside.

"It leads to an air shaft that lets out on Elizabeth Street. I really gotta run." Placing a finger under my chin and tilting my head up, Sally added, "If you want to scrape some of the shit off the table into an extra bonus, it's okay. Liquor's under the sink."

As soon as he left I found a bottle of Bacardi and some orange juice that appeared to be okay. After gulping half the drink at once, I finished the line he'd cut for me before. My ears were ringing from the intensity of so much, so fast. I was surprised at the steadiness of my hands as I got to work. It was relaxing, in a decadent sort of way. I felt a rush of power at having so much coke in front of me, touching my hands. There were people who would kiss my feet for what I had in front of me, and people who would kill for it.

The only thing that interrupted my reverie was the almost constant ringing of the phone. I wondered how much money Sally was losing by not being available for one short hour. At one point the phone rang about twenty times before the caller hung up. I felt bad for him or her, and hoped the person was calling from a car phone and not standing in the cold snow, leaning over the bum on the corner.

Several minutes later, as I was cutting a line for myself and finishing my second drink, I heard a pounding on the door. Oh my God! My heart started racing. What should I do? What the hell was I doing here? Oh God, I hope it's not a bust! Maybe it's the Mafia. I hoped so—I probably knew most of them and maybe could smile myself free. Should I put the coke away, under the sink maybe? Flush it? What if it wasn't the bad guys or the cops? I couldn't just flush like a million dollars of drugs without permission.

The banging on the door continued, and I was still running around the studio apartment like a total idiot. All I wanted to do was go to a nice college upstate, or maybe in New England. Why was this happening to me?

I finally scurried into the bathroom and shut the door behind me. Moving the hamper aside, I almost forgot about the TV surveillance screen. Glancing into it, I leaned closer at what looked like a familiar face. Oh God, he's not looking for me, is he? How would he know I was here?

I sank onto the floor and covered my ears to shut out the banging sound. Go away, I thought, staring at the screen. Go away, Mickey!

Chapter Twenty-Eight

I end up having to go back to Sally's three fucking times, and it's really pissing me off. I mean, does he want his fucking money, or what? Finally, at four, he's in. Meanwhile, I'm soaked from the goddamn snow, and I can barely move my fingers to hold the rolled-up twenty he passes me.

After I snort two big lines, my nose starts to bleed. Shit! It's embarrassing.

Passing me a crumpled napkin from the counter, Sally goes, "You better watch it, Mickey-boy. You're not going to make any money if you keep using up the profits. You gotta reinvest."

Oh yeah, I think, like there's not a big coke booger hanging out of *your* nose right now! Everyone's a critic. Everyone can handle it but *me,* right? You all got to try and control *my fucking life*!

"Oh yeah, I saw your sister last night," Sally says. "She's something else!"

Something about this skeavy shit with boogers sticking out of his nose and a pock-marked face talking about Catherine is more than I can take. I reach for an empty rum bottle and I'm going to swing it when the light over the front door starts flashing. Sally is pushing me into the bathroom before I can make my move and kick his ass.

"Joey!" he says when he opens the door. "Brother, am I glad to see you! You hear about the bust at the Pit . . ."

I'm about to step out of the bathroom and tell Joey what the piece of shit said about Catherine, when I hear the front door slam open.

"Freeze!" I hear.

"Cops?" Sally says in a squeaky voice.

And I'm outta there. There's an escape hatch near the floor in the bathroom, and faster than I ever moved before, I'm wiggling on my belly out into the alley. I don't stop running until I get to the subway at Prince Street, and then I ride the R train for four hours, and I can't stop shaking. It's eight o'clock in the morning when I realize that I still have Sally's money stuffed into my underwear, so I sneak to Catherine's school, figuring the first thing I should do is pay her back. I think about kicking her ass for ever knowing Sally, but then *she'd* know that *I* know Sally. And besides, I have a score to settle with a certain mutual "friend" in Brooklyn. Joey is gonna have to come up with some good stories to cover his ass if he really is a fink, or worse, an actual cop. First I'll try to find Frankie. He always knows what to do, and anyway he might spot me some rock.

*f*rankie charges me almost double the going price and then has the nerve to say he'll "look into it" when I tell him about last night. So I slug him and run. Stupid pussy wasn't gonna do a fucking thing. What a chickenshit little snot-nosed wannabe.

Why are people always fucking with me?

Chapter Twenty-Nine

The deal I made with God was that okay, yes, I would do coke that day, but after finishing this last packet from Sally, I wouldn't do any more until, maybe, graduation.

My heart raced through two back-to-back episodes of *Charlie's Angels* on cable and one episode of *Matlock,* where the mob blows up Ben Matlock's car. It grew harder to focus on TV as the day wore on. At least I seemed to have digested the egg sandwich, so I had some food in me.

The loneliness became overwhelming during commercial breaks, and I thought of renting a video. But Pop would be home soon, if he didn't go out drinking again, so it would be best for me to get out of the house.

My hand was shaking as I picked up the phone and dialed Joey's number. Maybe he could help me get through this Mickey thing. He always seemed to care. I imagined the scent of garlic mixed with his aftershave as the phone rang at his house in Bensonhurst. As I wondered why he never kissed me on the lips, the phone rang for the twelfth time. After sixteen rings I hung up.

It took me about twenty minutes to fix my makeup and to find subway fare.

By the time I left, school was out at St. Patrick's, and I wished again that I could be one of the girls whose legs must be freezing under their plaid skirts. Even as dirty gray slush splattered their knee socks, they looked happier than me. They looked like they would be going home to families that would be together on Thanksgiving.

The sky was ugly, and it would probably snow again soon, but I didn't turn back. Down on the subway platform, as I waited for the B train to Bensonhurst, I tore little threads of yarn from my mittens to keep from bugging out. I was pissed off at the bitch in the Korean deli— Erica and I called it the Orange Deli because of its big orange awning—because she wouldn't sell me a sixteen-ounce can of beer. I began to wish I'd taken Erica with me, because she had fake ID.

I sneezed. Pacing the platform, I wondered if anyone thought I was acting funny. Could they tell by seeing me walk that I was coked up, scared and miserable? Would Joey make me feel better? I promised myself to tell him the truth about my pathetic life so he could help me out. He was older, he'd know what to do. He'd fix everything.

When the train finally came, I was lucky enough to find a seat. Putting my Walkman on, I sang along in my head to Melissa Etheridge's second album. I closed my eyes, which normally I wouldn't do on the subway, but it was early enough that the train was crowded, and probably no one would try to rob me.

Although I tried to lose myself in the music coming through my headphones, I couldn't help counting the stops, which seemed to come painfully slow. My foot tapped, and I pinched the skin between my thumb and hand to keep my stomach from bunching up in my belly.

By the time the train stopped at Seventy-ninth Street in Bensonhurst, I was feeling better. Although I knew I was still a little fucked up, I felt clearheaded and didn't think I was going to spew my guts out any second. Desperately wanting some fresh air, I ignored the pay phone on the platform and stumbled up to the street. Someone was using the phone on the corner, so I began walking toward Joey's. I'd never been inside his house, but he'd showed me where it was when we went out for dinner that first night. I had to walk slowly because the snow was deeper here than in Manhattan. The sidewalks that had been shoveled were now slippery with a thin coat of ice. Passing the restaurant where Joey and I had eaten, I stopped and gazed fondly inside for a moment. Soon the biting wind forced me to move on. Even with mittens on and my hands stuffed into the pockets of my leather jacket, the tips of my fingers stung from the cold.

I got all the way to Joey's house without finding a pay phone, so I just went up the front steps and rang the doorbell. There was a light on inside, so even though no one answered the bell, I tried knocking. Looking back, I see that I should've realized I was too high on coke and gone home then. Why else, except if I was wasted, would I bang on Joey's door, when he didn't even want me to *call* him at home because of his "business."

The door opened a crack. I gasped.

"Catherine, what the fuck are you doing here? Go home!"

I stared at my brother through the crack. He had a gun in his hand.

"Are you in trouble?" I whispered. "Want me to get the cops?"

Mickey laughed. "They're probably on their

205

way already," he said, "knowing our friend Joey."

"Mickey, what's happening?" I asked warily. I hoped he knew how to use that thing. Right now it was pointed at his foot.

"Just go home, okay? I can handle it."

From inside I heard something heavy fall over.

"Shit!" Mickey said, and moved quickly back inside. Although he shut the door, I didn't hear the lock turn, so I gently turned the handle, and sure enough, I could get in. For a second I considered running, but if something happened to Mickey . . . I knew I had to see that he was okay.

"Mickey, what the fuck are you doing? Give me the goddamn gun, you fucking idiot!" I shouted.

Mickey was pointing his gun at Joey, who was lying sideways on the floor, tied with a bedsheet to a chair. Evidently he hadn't been tied well, because one arm was already free.

"Cat, get the fuck outta here. This ain't your business!" Mickey said. His voice was shaking worse than his hands.

"Cathy, talk to him. He's crazy. You gotta do something," Joey said. His voice wasn't shaking at all. In fact, he sounded almost bored, which was funny for a man who had a gun pointed—kind of—at him.

"Mickey, what are you doing? Come on, let's go home, okay?" I said, trying to sound as cool as Joey.

"He's a fucking snitch!" Mickey screamed. "Maybe even a cop!"

I noticed then that Mickey's stuff—clothes, underwear, his worn Heather Locklear poster—were scattered around the room, which appeared to be a spare bedroom. The sofa was a pull-out. It was folded up, but the cushions weren't on it. I could see that it had been used recently as a bed.

Now I was pissed. "My brother's been living with you, and you never told me?" I said to Joey, walking closer. I was tempted to kick him in the forehead.

"Cathy, sweetheart, I haven't seen you in like two weeks!" he argued.

Well, whose fault is that?

Mickey shoved me aside as Joey began to pull at the sheet with his free hand. "Don't move!" he said shrilly. Then, to me, he said, "You remember that bust at Snakepit? Do you know that Joey was the only one who didn't get fucked?"

"It wasn't—" Joey started, but Mickey cut him off.

"Shut the fuck up!" he said to Joey. Then to me, "And now there's cops all over Mario's club—did you notice that?"

I hadn't noticed. I wondered if Mickey'd been doing drugs all day too. Like brother, like sister. At least it had been a while since I'd done my last line—the train ride alone was forty minutes, and the walk from Seventy-ninth Street took another fifteen. I figured I was much more capable of holding that gun than my brother. I reached for it.

"Why don't you give me the gun to hold?" I said gently. "I won't let him go, I promise."

Mickey pulled the gun back toward him. "I gotta think. I gotta figure this out. You know Sally was busted last night?"

I cringed and felt cold in my chest.

"Joey was there. Tell her about it, buddy," Mickey said, still waving the gun around.

"I swear, I won't let him go," I said as I reached for the gun again, although that was probably the first thing I would do. At least I'd make Mickey untie him. It was stupid to leave him lying there, especially if Mickey was wrong about Joey. My guess was that no matter what happened, Mickey's mobster career was over. I wondered if he knew it yet. In any case, it looked like Joey was helping me after all, in a backward sort of way.

Mickey stepped back. I reached for the gun again, and this time it seemed like he was going to give it to me. But before he could, there was a loud pounding at the door, and Mickey spun around quickly. His foot caught mine, and we went down. The loudest sound I'd ever heard suddenly filled my ears, and I wondered if I'd been shot, or if the front door had been broken down.

It turned out to be neither. The pounding on the front door continued, mixed with muffled shouts I couldn't make out. My ears were ringing, and I couldn't hear too well. I smelled something funny, kind of smoky and greasy at the same time. It struck me that someone must've been shot. My eyes were squeezed shut, and I didn't want to open them as I rolled over something sticky on the rug. I hoped it was just melted snow and dirt from where I'd been standing, dripping, a minute before.

Not until Joey lifted me off the floor and led me to the couch did I open my eyes. I guess I knew from the moment I heard the gun fire what had happened, but even as I sat on the couch looking at it while Joey went to the front door, I didn't want to believe that it was Mickey on the floor. His hands were pressed against his thigh, and his jeans were stained red.

The cops who came in then obviously knew Joey pretty well, but I no longer cared if Mickey was right about Joey being a cop too.

I was feeling more in control as I rushed back to the floor and knelt beside Mickey. He was lying on his side and breathing in shallow, quick breaths. But his eyes were open, even if they were glassy. At least he was alive.

"Remember when we were kids, and I used to be in a fight with one of the bigger boys, and you would always jump on his back or somethin', and pull his hair until he quit fighting me?" Mickey whispered.

I nodded as I wiped his forehead and smoothed his hair. My other hand pressed against his where they were trying to slow down the flow of blood from his leg.

"When you ever gonna let me fight for myself?" he said.

Chapter Thirty

Mickey moved back home after he got out of the hospital. Soon after, he moved out again; then, around Christmas, he moved back in with us. Ma and Pop were more generous after the accident.

The last Friday in January, I hurried home from school, like I did every day now. I'd applied for early admission to Bard College, and I kept expecting to hear. I would miss Erica, who was planning to go to Hunter College, in the city, but Bard wasn't too far away. She kept saying that when she got a Harley, she'd visit me every weekend.

Mickey was sitting at the kitchen table with his bad leg up on a chair and his cane leaning against the wall behind him. He was reading the paper—it was supposed to be the Help Wanteds, but I knew he was probably reading the comics.

"Hey, Cat, how's school?" he said, looking up.

I shrugged. "I'm almost done with that writing I'm doing for the yearbook."

"That's cool," Mickey said. He talked to me

a lot more now that Frankie and his crew wouldn't even walk on the same side of the sidewalk as him. Even though he practically *shot* Joey, Mickey would always be "the cop's friend" in the neighborhood. God, I hated thinking about Joey. It still hurt.

"Hey, guess what?" Mickey said before I could get to the table by the stairs, where the mail was stacked every day.

"What?" I said, sighing. I felt bad that he didn't have any mobster buddies anymore, but then, neither did I. At least I was getting on with my life. Especially because I wasn't ever going to be Mrs. Valentino, I could pretend I'd never known Joey.

"I think I wanna be a chef," he said. "There's this course I read about that's only two thousand dollars if I get in. You think you could put in a good word with Ma for me? You know I like to cook."

I sat at the table and leaned my forehead against my hand in frustration, although I couldn't help smiling. Mickey would never change.

"I thought you were going to be an engineer, because you like planning things," I said.

He shrugged and lit a cigarette with one hand while he flipped through pages in the paper with the other. "I just wanna keep my options open," he said. "I can't help it if I don't have everything planned out as good as you."

I started to stand up. Mickey said, "Joey called again today. You should call him. He just wants to apologize."

I shrugged. "For what? For being a cop? Why should he apologize for that? Or does he want me to forgive him for *lying* to me? Or maybe just for *using* me. I should've known when he kept asking me all those questions and wouldn't even give me a real kiss."

"I don't need to know about your love life. Anyway, I think we should be thankful, in a way," Mickey said. "I could be in jail right now if it weren't for him. He saved my ass by not bringing me in. I could be in jail right now."

"So *you* forgive him!" I said. "Anyway, now that he's back in L.A., what's the difference?"

Mickey stared at me for a while, but he didn't press the issue.

I grabbed the newspaper from Mickey, crinkling the edges in my fingers as I stared hard and angry at the comics. Suddenly I really wanted a line of coke, even though I hadn't done any since Christmas, when Erica first got her new cocaine connection. Believe it or not, she met her new dealer at the absolutely legitimate coffee bar in the East Village where we were now working. No matter where I went, I couldn't get away.

I pushed the paper back to Mickey and slowly headed upstairs. When I got there, I sat at my desk and turned on the computer I'd gotten with money I'd saved, Christmas money, and a loan from Ma. The amber letters of a story I'd started shined brightly in the dim light. I wondered how I could fit Mickey, Erica and Joey into the story, which was about an ex-mobster who was now homeless on the streets of New York.

"Cat!" Mickey yelled from downstairs.

"Whaddya want?" I yelled back, annoyed.

"Doncha want your mail?"

I forgot! Running downstairs, I almost tripped. Mickey stood at the bottom, leaning on his cane and wagging a long, white envelope. I grabbed for it, and he pulled it back.

"What's the name of that school you want to go to?" he said.

"Gimme that!"

"Was it . . . Bard College?" he teased, holding the letter too high for me to reach.

I was laughing. "Mickey, I swear, I'll knock you down."

"Sorry, but it says here that you didn't get

in," he said, holding the envelope up against the hall light as he hobbled backward into the den.

"Mickey! Give me the fucking letter!"

"Keep it down!" Pop yelled from his bedroom. "I'm trying to sleep."

"Mickey, please?" I whispered, and he tossed the envelope at me.

As I tore it open, he leaned over my shoulder. I tried to shield it with my hand so he couldn't see, but I was too excited and nervous to try hard.

"Oh my God!" I screeched, not caring what Pop had to say. "I got in! I have to call Erica!"

Mickey stopped me, a big grin on his face.

"Congratulations," he said. "I always knew you'd make it out of here first."

He pulled me close with one hand and wrapped his arm around me in a big hug. I didn't want him ever to let go. Suddenly I wondered why I was in such a hurry to leave home and the neighborhood. Sometimes it wasn't so bad. You always knew where to find someone who cared.

Shelley Stoehr is a dancer, choreographer and massage therapist. She is also the author of the acclaimed *Crosses* and *Weird on the Outside.* Shelley lives in San Francisco with her photographer husband, Mark Buhler.